Montgomery!

Who'd have thought they would end up congratulating their new pet for being disobedient?

By Josefine Beaumont

WHEN I awoke, that cold day in February, it seemed such an ordinary day. But that was before I found out that Montgomery was not only about to enter my home, but my life as well.

Mornings are a bit hectic in our house, but then, I suppose they are in most homes.

My husband, Bob, only ever had the time and inclination for a cup of coffee before departing for the office. Then after a habitual peck on the cheek and a cheery wave of the hand he'd be gone.

Then came the bit I dreaded.

What is it about kids in the morning anyway!

My three slept like logs. In fact, I sometimes thought that were the house to fall apart around their beds, they would carry right on snoring.

Our 16-year-old daughter, Tracey, walked about as though her eyelids were glued together, and both 14-year-old Ian and six-year-old Hazel were human tortoises. Every morning found me urging them to get a move on, especially Hazel, who was picked up early by the primary school mini-bus.

It was a relief when the door closed on the last of them. Love them as I do, it was still exhausting getting them off to school.

As any mother knows, housework takes up most of the day.

Tracey's bedroom looked as though a cyclone had passed through it in the night.

It was such a pretty room, too. Or it used to be! We had covered the walls in a pretty floral wallpaper, because that's what she had wanted.

Goodness only knows why we bothered, because every available inch was taken up with posters of George Clooney. He stared down at me from every given angle, and I sighed wearily.

What it was to be 16!

I was just about to wade through to Ian's room when I heard Jane call out.

Jane was our next-door neighbour. A small, sprightly woman of 65 years of age, her hair a halo of white and her eyes the bluest I had ever seen.

"You're early this morning," I said, glancing at the clock in the hall as I hurried downstairs. It was only 10.20. Jane and I usually had our coffee and a chat around 11.

Her eyes sparkled as she waved an air-mail envelope at me and cried, "I've had a letter from Thomas."

Thomas was her son and he lived in Melbourne.

"Oh, super," I said warmly.

"And you'll never guess," she said breathlessly, plumping down at the table, "but look . . ."

She tipped the contents of the envelope onto the table. A thick letter spilled out along with several colour photographs and an air ticket.

"Jane!" I gasped.

"I'm actually going, Sally," she said with wonderment in her voice. "I'm actually going to Australia. The extension to their house is finished and all ready for me to move into!"

Tears filled my eyes as I sat opposite her. Reaching over the table, I covered her hand with my own and said thickly, "I'll miss you, Jane. I'll really miss you."

"No more than I shall miss you," she murmured.

"You've been like a mother to me!" I wailed.

"And you've been like a daughter to me." She sniffed, and then we were grinning idiotically through our tears.

Wiping her eyes, she asked, "Tell me the truth, do you think I'm an old fool?"

"Of course not," I cried hotly.

"All that talk about me going out there . . ." she said. "It didn't seem real to me, you know, and now . . ." Her voice tailed away.

"You'll love it," I assured her.

"But uprooting at my age? Is it wise?"

"What's your age got to do with it?" I argued. "You talk as though you're in your dotage. And just think, you'll see all your grandchildren."

Her eyes filled with tears all over again. "I miss Thomas, you know. We were always close. He's a good son."

"He's a wonderful son," I said enthusiastically, thinking of all the letters, the photos, tapes and phone calls she had received over the past 11 years.

"So when do you go?" I asked, rising to make the coffee.

"On Friday the nineteenth," she announced proudly.

"Friday the nineteenth?" I gulped. "But . . . that's only two weeks away!"

"Well, you know Mr Preston made me an offer for the house? I telephoned him this morning and he's thrilled. He's got a mortgage all lined up. As for the contents, they don't amount to much. I can get one of those house clearance men in, but . . ."

"But what?" I prompted, placing the coffee mugs upon the table.

"It's Montgomery," she stated dolefully.

MONTGOMERY! I had forgotten about him. "What about Montgomery?" I asked her fearfully. "I daren't ask you," she whispered. I tell you my heart sank to my ankles. If Jane had a failing, then it came in the huge shape of Montgomery.

When I say that mutt was big, I mean big. He positively dwarfed poor Jane when she took him for walkies.

He was a Boxer dog, with the manners of a stray.

She had acquired him as a puppy from the RSPCA, and she simply adored him.

I don't believe that dog ever did a thing it was told. He was born unruly. He was neither a respector of persons — as the postman had found out to his cost — nor of property.

Montgomery thought nothing of audaciously sauntering into someone's garden, where he would proceed to energetically dig an enormously large hole, much to the fury of the irate owners of the garden, or leave a ghastly reminder of his visit.

Montgomery wouldn't lie on the floor. Oh no, he liked the cushioned depths of Jane's settee, and once ensconced, no amount of verbal threats nor sweet persuasion would move him.

I kept right on smiling. It was a wonder my face didn't crack. It all came out in a beseeching rush.

"Well, I wouldn't ask you, but I know you love him and so . . . so will you have him, Sally? Will you?

"I wouldn't want him to go to strangers and he . . . he likes you, really he does and I . . . I couldn't bear to have him put down! It would be like killing a friend. Please, Sally, say you'll have him."

I felt like collapsing on the floor in a heap at the prospect of giving a home to Montgomery.

Not that I didn't like him. He was so big and dozy, one couldn't help but like him.

But love him? The thing I loved about dear Montgomery was that he lived next door and not with me.

I told myself that this was some dreadful nightmare. That any minute now I would waken and find myself safe and warm cuddled next to Bob in bed.

But no, this was the cold light of day and Jane was saying anxiously, "I can't take him over to Australia . . ."

"Of course I'll take him . . ."

*　　*　　*　　*

"Are you mad?" Bob stared at me from across the dinner table.

"What else could I do?" I shouted defiantly.

"You could have told her we didn't want him!"

"Well, I didn't! And neither would you have done had she asked you, and you know it!"

Bob sighed wearily. "It's insane, that dog."

"He's lovely and cuddly," Hazel said indignantly.

"And he's friendly. I've always wanted a dog," Ian put in excitedly.

"He's gross." Tracey shuddered.

"Can he sleep on my bed?" Ian asked hopefully.

"No!" Bob and I chorused in unison.

I shared my look between the bright faces of my kids and said firmly, "There'll be no sleeping on beds for that dog. When he comes into this house he'll do as he's told . . ."

SO that he could get used to living with us, Jane brought him around the next morning. She plonked his dog bed (unused) upon the floor. After a quick look about him, Montgomery leapt onto the settee.

"Oh, dearie me," Jane murmured helplessly. She cast me an apologetic glance and then, gingerly tapping his rear end, she said fondly, "Naughty, naughty boy. You mustn't lie there. Get down."

Montgomery half opened one eye and then shut the said eye.

"Oh dear," Jane murmured again.

"Down, boy!" I yelled, making Jane jump.

She threw me a reproachful look. "I'll leave you to it, dear," she said tearfully, and departed hastily.

Left alone with Montgomery, I poked him in the ribs and said firmly, "Now, boy, down you go. Do you hear me? Down!"

But Montgomery was having none of it. Montgomery had no intentions of getting down. He had never, ever, done as he was told and he wasn't about to start now.

So, wrapping my arms around his thick neck, I dragged him on to the floor. It was like shifting an elephant.

He gave me an indignant look then promptly leapt back onto the settee.

Grim faced, I fetched Bob's slipper and waggled it before his eyes.

He gave it an interested look, decided it wasn't edible, and shut his eyes.

"Down, boy, down!" I yelled hysterically.

But it was no use, so I gave in, and left him snoring loudly while I went to make the tea.

Jane had also brought a list with her. It was a list of his likes concerning food and it was as long as my arm. And heading that list was best steak, followed by bacon, followed by smoked haddock.

"Best steak?" I had stared at Jane.

"He likes best steak," she had replied defiantly.

Don't we all?

"You'll have tinned dog food and like it," I now told him.

Montgomery's face fell. But I didn't care!

*　　*　　*　　*

Jane departed on a Friday amidst tears and promises to write. I cried all the way home from the airport.

Her last anxious words to me had been, "Don't forget dear Montgomery, will you?" Was she kidding?

Forget Montgomery? Was it possible to do so?

I should be so lucky!

*　　*　　*　　*

Doubtless you have heard all the jokes about dogs taking their owners for a walk. Well, with Montgomery it was no joke.

Once attached to a lead he hurtled full steam ahead. And boy, was he enthusiastic and full of energy!

"My right arm will end up a foot longer than my left arm," I complained to Bob one night in bed.

Being a man, he laughed. I took offence at that. How could he be so callous?

Only that very morning Montgomery, his tongue hanging out with joy, had yanked me along the road at an alarmingly fast pace.

A young boy with a group of friends had shouted derisively, "We have lift off!"

They had all howled with laughter. My face had burned bright lobster red with humiliation.

Montgomery, with his great muddy feet that reminded me of two dinner plates dipped in sludge, was a constant embarrassment. I just couldn't figure out what Jane had seen in this great oaf! Love is truly blind! But, every time I thought of what Montgomery considered normal behaviour, I cringed in mortification!

He jumped up at me when I shouted sit but had to be forced out of doors at night, so that I wouldn't face a puddle come the morning.

He was as greedy a beast as one could ever come across and as arrogant and self-willed as a donkey.

He hogged the fire, hogged the settee and even bounded defiantly upstairs to plonk himself down on Ian's bed, then howled when Bob marched him right back down again as if he was being ill-treated.

How I longed for Montgomeryless days. I could hardly remember that glorious time in the past when we'd been like any other, normal family. But how normal would we stay with Montgomery with us?

SUDDENLY he had been with us three weeks — though it seemed much longer — and we were into March. There had been a sudden fall of snow that iced over, but despite that, the sun shone and there was no excuse to abandon Montgomery's morning hurl around the fields.

I paused, breathless, upon the humped-backed bridge that spanned the local river. Several mothers with prams and toddlers were about. The children were wrapped against the cold, their faces wind-stung and shining with happiness and innocence.

There's something extraordinarily beautiful about the awkward yet graceful movements of a small child. I watched entranced as they merrily skipped and tumbled into the snow.

I smiled to myself. Bob and I had spent many a happy hour down by that river with our own brood.

Then Montgomery began straining at the leash. My arm felt as if it was about to part with its socket and I was just about to continue haphazardly on my way.

Then it happened.

One small boy, head covered in a woolly red cap, chubby legs encased in bright blue trousers, was skipping dangerously near the embankment.

I saw his mother's alarmed face, her heavily-pregnant body lurch forwards, her mouth open to call him back.

One minute he was there and the next he was skidding down the bank. There was a splash and he was gone.

Shock surged through me . . . But before I knew it I'd let go of the leash, shouted to Montgomery, to "stay," and climbed onto the bridge.

Before I hit the water there was a last glimpse of the boy's mother as she sank on to her knees in the snow, her mouth frozen into a soundless scream.

I hit the water full force and when it covered my head I was plunged into darkness.

I STILL have nightmares. About the ice cold; about the bursting pain in my lungs; the way the water crept insidiously through my clothes until they were sodden and heavy and dragging me down. I wake up crying, arms flaying as they had in that river. I wake shuddering, remembering as I do the moment my grasping fingers latched on to the boy's coat, and how it seemed that I was down there for ever.

I recall thinking we weren't going to make it. We aren't going to make it! Dear God, help us!

And then something was grasping my coat collar with strong teeth. My free hand was clinging to Montgomery's coat as he forged strongly upwards. Up where the air was clear; out from under that watery horror.

And then we surfaced.

After that, everything became a jumble of voices, faces and happenings.

A man waded into the water to assist us. Willing hands reached out. But even then Montgomery wouldn't let go.

Not until we lay safely upon a bed of snow did he release his grip on my collar and began to furiously lick my face.

I remember the hot, hot tears falling on to my cold, cold face. A voice crying pitifully over and over, "You saved my son's life . . . you saved my son's life . . . you and that dog . . . how could I ever thank you . . . how can I ever thank you . . .?"

It was at that precise moment that Montgomery's long tongue rasped against my face.

"Stop that!" I automatically commanded.

And then I passed out.

WE made the national newspapers, Montgomery and I. I sent a copy of all the cuttings to Jane who promptly phoned me, all tears and joy. "Dear Montgomery," she sniffed over the phone. "And I was so afraid he'd be a nuisance. He is rather wilful," she admitted grudgingly.

I cast a glance to where Montgomery was sprawled on the settee and I closed my eyes.

"I have to go now, Jane," I told her. "It's time for Montgomery's dinner."

"Very well, dear, 'bye for now."

"'Bye, Jane," I replied.

"What exactly is he having for dinner?" she asked anxiously and hurriedly before I replaced the receiver.

I stole a look at Montgomery, who shuffled his great backside deeper into the cushions.

And I smiled to myself.

"Best steak," I replied gently, then put down the phone. ∎

In-Laws I

**They had tried to give
the newly-weds
everything —
except the luxury
of living their
own lives.**

I THINK you're worrying needlessly." Tom tried to reassure Harriet, but she wasn't convinced. She passed him back his road map. "And I think we should go," she persisted. Then her tone softened into the coaxing one, which over their years of marriage had always melted down his objections and remoulded his ideas into her own.

"They're so young . . ." she tried again.

"Kids marry young these days — and besides," Tom reminded her, "we were the same age as them when we got married."

"Exactly," Harriet said. She didn't have to say more for, after 25 years together, her mind was the only thing left he could still read without his glasses . . .

He could remember clearly enough their early days — days when the romance of courtship had turned into the cold hard slog of reality. They'd both worked, earning as much as they could to save up for new furniture as replacements for the hand-me-downs donated from both families.

Trouble!

By
Suzanne
Thorpe

There were days — months — when they were often too tired for even a goodnight kiss; when their hopes to start a family went unvoiced because they just had to replace that second-hand cooker first, that dodgy washer, that worn-out settee . . .

"I see what you mean," he murmured. "Marriage could come as a rude awakening to Claire, after her time at art school with you playing cook and me playing chauffeur. And our son-in-law seems a bit of a dreamer to me."

"Paul is a commercial artist, dear," Harriet tactfully corrected.

"Hmmm . . ." Tom was thinking that in his day men used to be plumbers or carpenters, bricklayers or machine operators. They did men's jobs. But drawing pictures . . .

"And I've been thinking," Harriet went on, aiming her final shot. "Those rose bushes you gave them to start their garden off . . ."

Tom's rapt attention was at last seized.

"Well, Paul's bound to have neglected them, isn't he? After all, what would an artist know about gardening?"

Harriet sat back in her armchair, pretending interest in her knitting as she waited for Tom to take the bait. It took just two knits and a purl . . .

She was right, Tom thought. What would a young man who earned a living drawing pictures know about treating roses with phostrogen in showery weather, shielding them from pests and pruning back old blooms to make strong new shoots?

He opened the road map and Harriet smiled to herself.

C LAIRE was frowning in thought.

"I think you're worrying needlessly," Paul said.

"You did hear what I said? Mum rang my office this morning. She and Dad want to come down for a week!"

"Fine," Paul said, tucking heartily into his carefully-prepared lunch.

"But we've only been married eight weeks," Claire reminded him ruefully.

"Well, your folk won't interfere," Paul said.

Claire looked down at her untouched salad, thinking that Paul didn't know her parents as well as she did. As an only child they had always been a little over-protective. Now they had gained a "son" that care would extend to him, too.

No, they wouldn't interfere, they were more likely to try to help the love-birds nest a little more comfortably.

That's what worried her . . .

"It's rather small," Harriet said, as her sharp eyes took in every inch of the cottage.

"It's just what we wanted," Claire replied.

"Well, perhaps Dad and I can buy you a new dining table to replace that old thing?"

"Yes!" Tom echoed eagerly.

Claire and Paul exchanged worried glances.

14

"That's an antique," Claire explained. "We like old things."

Harriet's face registered confusion. "But I've spent all my married life trying to get new ones!" she said, dismayed at this strange way of thinking.

Claire rallied the situation quickly. "Paul and I want to take you both out to dinner tonight!"

"Yes —" Paul chimed in.

"But that costs money," Harriet objected.

"A sandwich will do fine," Tom added. "You really shouldn't —"

"We insist," Paul said.

Claire and Paul had made the right decision on a restaurant, having deliberated on it for a week beforehand. Claire's instructions were that it had to serve traditional English food on its menu, with no concealed lighting — or else Dad wouldn't be able to read the menu — and have no piped music in the background or else Mum would be asking the waiter to turn it down because she couldn't hear herself gossip.

Paul had found such a suitable place — the Manor. It was an old country house converted into a hotel and restaurant just outside town.

Harriet and Tom seemed happy enough with it, and were as chirpy as two canaries — at least until the waiter came to take their order.

"Vegetarian!" Harriet exclaimed, her eyes round with shock over her menu. "But you've never been vegetarian before, Claire! Why the change?"

Claire looked uncomfortable.

"We wanted to try it . . ."

Harriet looked at her daughter as if she had just been betrayed.

Tom gallantly stepped in to fill the silence. "We'll have the roast beef," he told the waiter.

"And two ratatouille," Paul added.

The conversation at the table seemed to taper off then . . .

Harriet and Tom assured Claire and Paul that they would be quite happy to "potter around" whilst the couple were out at work. But, secretly, Tom was desperate to tidy up the garden while Harriet had her eye on what she considered a sparse and badly-organised larder . . .

That evening when Claire and Paul arrived home, their driveway looked different. There were no dandelions, litter, and not a trace of weeds . . .

Tom was surveying his handiwork and looked up when they approached.

Claire was concerned to see his face looking tired beneath the grin. "You've been doing too much," she said, planting a kiss on his hot cheek.

"But it all looks very nice," Paul added tactfully.

"You really shouldn't have though, Dad . . ."

"Wait until you see what your mother's done in the house!" Tom announced proudly.

Panic chased over Claire's face as she dashed indoors.

The same picture of perfection met her. The pine Welsh dresser shone like a golden mirror, the tiled floor winked at her, and crystal flower vases sparkled.

"A good, old-fashioned, blue bag in the white wash!" her mother said, as Claire stared at the curtains. Then Claire's eyes dropped to the kitchen table.

The surface was covered with at least a dozen plates of baking — Cornish pasties, sausage rolls, queen cakes, jam and curd tarts, all with the white flour she and Paul had replaced with wholemeal, the jams and curds they had replaced with organic honey, and the meat they had cut out completely.

But she knew her mother would never understand that.

"You really shouldn't have . . ." Paul's voice sounded constricted as he appeared at her elbow.

"It's no bother," Harriet said, her face looking tired but happy. "You two need feeding up!"

BY the third day of their stay, Harriet and Tom had dug, tidied, trimmed, cleaned and polished everything that wasn't perfection. Hints that they "really shouldn't have" went unheeded because they, in their goodness, believed they were helping two young newlyweds who worked long hours at their jobs.

Efforts to distract — suggestions of trips to a matinée or to a nearby wildlife park — were declined on the grounds of contentment and exhaustion.

So Claire and Paul felt guilt-ridden and on edge.

"I'd like to go downstairs for a glass of milk," Paul said that night in their bedroom.

"So why don't you?" Claire asked, bemused.

"Because I'm afraid if I go down while your mum's still up she'll want to iron my pyjamas — again!"

Claire put down the hairbrush she was using. "It's nearly the end of the week," she reminded him.

He got into bed and fell asleep without giving her his usual goodnight kiss.

Next morning, breakfast was an unusually silent one.

Harriet was worried.

"I hope they haven't had their first row," she said to Tom next morning as she watched them walk to the car. Usually they held hands and talked happily, but this morning they walked separately and silently.

Tom came and cupped her shoulders from behind with his big hands.

"Well, one thing's for sure," he murmured into her hair, "until they have they won't be truly married!"

Harriet spun around on him. "Tom!" she chastised.

He smiled tenderly down at her. "You know you look twenty again when you're a little angry. It makes your eyes glow!"

Harriet suppressed a smile. "Don't try to wriggle out of what you just implied about marriage being nothing but arguments."

"I implied no such thing," Tom said. "I meant no marriage, however happy, will be free of disagreements. It's solving them that brings you closer, not evading them."

Harriet conceded that point and let Tom lead her through to the garden. She felt him slip an arm around her shoulders.

"Can you remember our first row?" he asked.

She shook her head, but she did really, and he knew she did.

"As I recall," he went on, "it was all over something as ridiculous as a jar of blackcurrant jam. You had that pretty nose out of joint for a week because my mother had made it for us and you said it made you less of a woman or something. You were rather tearful and incoherent about it as I remember . . ."

He felt her shoulders shaking gently, and peering around the curl of hair which had demurely fallen over her cheek he saw that she was laughing and he began to chuckle, too.

"And we've broken that golden rule, too, haven't we, love? We've crossed that line between love and interference . . ."

Harriet looked up at him, a protest burning on her lips. "But —"

He laid a finger gently across them as a seal. "And you know what we have to do?"

Harriet thought of the rug she had seen in the nearby High Street — it would have started their empty box room off perfectly, and the chutney she had planned to make that day . . .

"Yes," she said. "I know."

O N entering the cottage, Claire and Paul were prepared to face one of Harriet's traditional English menus, were prepared for anything in the garden from a gazebo to an ornamental pool, were prepared to be assailed by the smell of lemon polish . . . but as they walked from the car a chocolate wrapper cartwheeled over the drive, and Claire noticed a rogue weed in the flower bed.

Paul noticed the vague lack of perfection about the place which was explained when they tried the cottage door and found it locked.

They exchanged puzzled glances, looks which said, "They can't possibly have gone out, can they . . . ?"

Indoors, the pleasant absence of smell greeted them. There was no polish to veil the air, no baking smells . . .

"Paul!" Claire cried, as she ran through to the kitchen. She hadn't needed to call him though, for he was hot on her heels.

In the kitchen they both stopped dead, their eyes wide, their mouths just a little agape. Here was the last remaining trace of Harriet and Tom. A casserole dish of ratatouille all ready for the oven, a loaf of granary bread, a bottle of white wine freshly chilled, and a bunch of long-stemmed roses.

Paul lifted the bevelled-edged card which slanted across them. Harriet had written it and both had signed. It said simply:

We shouldn't have — we really shouldn't! Have a happy marriage, Harriet and Tom.

"Have we got a message?" Claire asked, trying to peer over his shoulder. Paul tossed the card back on the table and looped his arms around her waist.

"No, love," he said, smiling. "Your mum and dad have got the message — we've still got the honeymoon . . ." ■

The Deer

by Joyce Stranger

Inspired by an illustration by Mark Viney

In the shadowy woods the young deer play,
Happily frisk through the dappled day.
'Neath the trees behind them, their mothers dream,
They bask, they feed, they drink from the stream.
Alone on the hills the great stags stand,
Looking down on their promised land.
Horn buds in velvet, the stags all know
They must wait till new antlers grow.
Restless, fretful, they rub against trees,
Read the news that is borne on the breeze.
At last each stag, in proud array
Bellows his challenge throughout the day.
The hills re-echo with roar and crash
As the fighting monarchs their antlers clash.
The victors step proud down the mountainsides,
To seek in the woods their waiting brides.
As the stags join the herd, the little ones stare.
They've never seen such majesty there.
Winter strikes chill and ices the burn.
With Spring, the stags to the hills return.
In dappled sunlight and breaking dawn,
Once more in the woods are the little ones born.

By Suzanne
Thorpe

ATTRACTION
OPPOSITES

Their problem was they had nothing in common — except their love for each other.

THEY were the ideal couple — grey-haired, about 60, with round faces like shiny apples, and looked as if they had been married for so many years their coat sleeves had woven together. They were just what Sally needed to complete her quota.

"Excuse me!" she called out. "Would you mind answering a few questions for market research?"

They paused, turning from the shop window to give her a smile.

"What's it all about?" the man asked.

Sally's clipboard quivered with anticipation and because of the sharp, October air. This was her "married couple, 60 or over," this was her quota finished, this would lead to a mug of hot chocolate with her feet up on the sofa!

"It's about holidays," she told them. "Could I have your names, please?"

"George and Lavinia Meadowcroft!" they both offered eagerly.

"And are you over sixty?" Sally asked.

"Only just," George said, with a wink. "My back and legs are, but the rest of me feels twenty-one!"

Lavinia gave a supportive chuckle, and Sally felt encouraged to go on.

"Do you take a holiday annually, more than that — or less?"

"Annually," they chorused.

"But not together," Lavinia added.

"Oh!" Sally's pen slipped. This was an unexpected development.

"George goes fishing in Scotland with his brother and I go to a water-colour group in the Cotswolds," Lavinia explained.

"Well, if you were to go together, what activities would you choose?"

"Fishing, of course," George said, without hesitation. "Darts and snooker, too."

"Don't forget your cricket, dear," Lavinia chipped in, adding, "And I like poetry, painting and music."

"Oh, right," Sally said, feeling as if her brain had slipped out of gear and was grating to find a new one.

"Do you prefer organised holidays through a travel agent, go-as-you-please ones — or ones not booked at all?"

"Not booked at all!" George chimed in.

"Organised through a travel agent," Lavinia said decisively.

By now, Sally should have known that.

She did guess correctly, though, that George's dream holiday would be canoeing down the Amazon, whilst Lavinia's was a coach tour of Europe, that Lavinia packed two days before and George at the last minute.

By the time the questionnaire was completed, Sally had lost quite a lot of faith in her three years' experience as a researcher and in her judgement of people.

GEORGE and Lavinia were certainly deceptive beneath their matching trenchcoats, their twinning pepper-and-salt hair, and their happy faces. Holiday-wise they seemed to rate zero in common, yet over 40 years of marriage — according to one question — meant they had to have something in common, but what?

It made her wonder if she and Steve would end up like that — taking separate holidays and having different interests? Yet, despite the holiday situation, the Meadowcrofts did seem happy together.

The Meadowcrofts cropped up again that evening, in conversation, when she was sharing a glass of wine and a peel-off face mask with her flat-mate, Jenny.

"Well, talking of odd couples, it beats me how you and Steve stick together," Jenny said, the wine loosening everything except the face masks.

Her remark hit home, right into a dark, cobwebbed corner of Sally's mind where she had buried the same doubt.

Although Steve had all the good points, such as honesty, patience and kindness (survey 83 for a marriage counselling group) in the day-to-day practicalities of life Sally found him absent-minded, untidy, unpunctual and often downright vexing.

He was her exact opposite. He was the logical, plodding bookworm whilst she was the impulsive, excitable canary.

"He didn't even send you flowers on Valentine's Day!" Jenny said indignantly.

"He did buy me a gold-plated pen," Sally excused him. "And in my job that's a very practical gift."

"Practical!" Jenny gasped, round-eyed and horrified, as if Sally had just uttered an obscene word. "What's that got to do with romance?"

Sally would have smiled — if the face mask hadn't been so tight — for Jenny wasn't the sort to go without flowers on Valentine's Day — or any other.

In one way, she was right — Steve didn't seem to fill all Sally's emotional needs. Yet if she were asked to fill in one of her own questionnaires and outline her ideal partner, what would she say? Someone with her own interests in romantic novels and knitting, her habits of collecting stray cats and worries?

Somehow Sally couldn't — didn't want to — picture such a man.

She couldn't picture the knight-on-the-white-charger type either, so where did that leave her? Squarely with Steve — always with kindness, sometimes with vexation, but never with romance.

"Well, I don't know what you should do," Jenny sighed in her mother-hen tone.

Neither did Sally, but the next day, some answers were on their way.

*   *   *   *

She was on a new project — pet food — and who should she run into in the High Street but George and Lavinia, arm in arm and smiling.

"Any more questions today?" George called out cheerily.

"Pet food!" Sally called back.

The couple wandered over.

"We can help there," Lavinia offered. "We have two cats and a dog."

On the subject of pets the Meadowcrofts were for once in agreement, although on the question of titbits Lavinia was stoical with her answer of "never", while George gave a more generous "sometimes".

"You look a bit peaky today," Lavinia said. "It's all this cold weather."

"Cold enough for two pairs of braces," George added, with his now-familiar wink.

"You wouldn't fancy sharing a pot of tea with us, would you?" Lavinia suggested. "We usually stop for one about now."

Sally didn't need asking twice and once inside the café she began to thaw out. With her shoes squeezed off under the table, a cup of steaming tea in front of her and butter oozing over a crumpet, she found herself pouring out her problems to the cheerful faces of George and Lavinia.

"You say Steve's a junior house doctor at the hospital?" Lavinia checked.

"Yes, but his bedside manner is definitely lacking!" Sally quipped ruefully.

"Well, doctors think that way, love," George assured her. "They think of hearts as pumps and flowers as inconveniences in wards!"

Sally nodded, having, to her own dismay, already discovered that.

"You see, I think a lot of him after two years, but to be honest —" she struggled to explain "— to be honest, lately I'm convinced we're just not compatible!"

THERE — it was out, like a stain on the white tablecloth, and she awaited supportive nods and groans of sympathy. She didn't expect laughter!

"Compatibility!" George said, chuckling. "That old myth!"

Lavinia admonished him gently, but Sally noticed she was smiling, too.

"Well, he hardly ever agrees with me over restaurants and clothes, or books and films," Sally protested in her own defence.

"All the important things," George teased.

Then he added with his mischievous wink, "Do you mean hardly ever, sometimes, always or never?"

Now it was Sally who had to laugh.

"You know, it's usually a case of opposites attracting," George went on. "Like a magnet and iron filings, nuts and bolts, sockets and screws. Take Vinny and me."

"Yes, I was wondering," Sally admitted. "Those separate holidays?"

"That's because we used to go together!" Lavinia explained. "George is one for joining in and I'm one for opting out, I'm afraid.

"He loved going in for all the competitions at the holiday camp we used to take the children to. You know — Mr Knobbly Knees and Yodeller Of The Week, that sort of thing."

"So what did you do?" Sally asked, intrigued.

"I hid under a big hat and dark glasses!"

Sally laughed again.

"But you've been married for over forty years!"

"Oh yes!" they agreed in gleeful unison.

"It's the old nuts and bolts," chimed in George. "Vinny's your china cup, sherry and ballet type, while I'm more your mug, beer and darts — but it works!"

Sally's head swam with bizarre images of loving-cups, champagne and romantic novels mingling with test tubes, lager and text-books.

"Yes," she agreed with her laughing companions.

But she had begun to feel decidedly odd, like Alice in Wonderland, having everything the wrong way around.

* * * *

That evening Steve rang.

"I've won the hospital raffle," he told Sally excitedly. "A holiday!"

"A holiday! Where to?"

"Well, that's just it." He sounded just a little sheepish. "We've got a choice."

Sally knew what he meant — they hardly ever agreed on where to go on a Saturday night out, let alone a holiday.

Then images of china cups and mugs, ballet and darts matches, flooded back to her. "What choices do we have?"

SALLY didn't see George and Lavinia again until well into November. She was walking down the High Street when she heard a familiar voice call out, "Any questions for us today?" Turning, she met those smiling faces — the trenchcoats interwoven as before.

"Not today, George," she greeted them with a smile. "I've a week off. We got engaged last night and we're going away for a few days' holiday to celebrate."

"Oh, lovely!" Lavinia cooed.

"This is to the young man who hardly ever agrees with you?" George checked.

"Well, I've had second thoughts," Sally said. "What did you call it, George? That old myth — compatibility? A couple of things decided me — the first was the raffle."

"Raffle?" George and Lavinia echoed, amazed.

"We won a holiday in one — only we had a choice of trips.

"So I agreed to the pony trekking in the New Forest, and Steve opted for the shopping trip to London."

"That's diplomatic," George said.

"That's love!" Lavinia corrected.

"So where are you going?" George asked, intrigued.

"Steve asked for the cash alternative — we're going to celebrate the engagement with my folk."

"That's nice," Lavinia said.

"Steve'll probably end up playing darts with my dad at the local, and I'll no doubt end up watching some old movies on TV with Mum," Sally admitted.

"That's understandable," Lavinia said.

"But it was probably survey number one hundred and twelve which really decided me," Sally went on.

"For a compatibility census?" George teased.

"For an insurance company — 'How would you like to spend your retirement years?' "

The tender look which passed between George and Lavinia spoke for itself. It said they wanted to spend them, quite simply, together.

"Well, I just knew that however I want to spend my retirement years, I want to spend them with Steve," Sally finished.

Lavinia gave Sally a kiss of congratulation, and George had some more advice for her.

"I hope you're not expecting him to change, though — I haven't!"

He was given a playful dig in the ribs by Lavinia.

"I'm banking on him not changing!" Sally laughed.

Looking at George and Lavinia, at their contagious happiness, she knew the love between Steve and her would be one and the very same — sometimes out of step, certainly never predictable, but always true. ■

ALL TIED UP!

FOR THE BRIDE

The gift of a wooden spoon is said to ensure future domestic harmony. We show you how to use ribbons to make a delightful and unusual bridal gift.

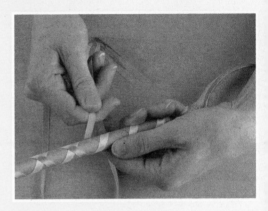

YOU WILL NEED

- wooden spoon
- gold water-based paint
- paintbrush
- gold gauze ribbon
- needle and thread
- scissors
- a selection of cream and gold satin ribbons
- pink and cream fabric flowers
- good luck charm

1 Paint the spoon. Bind the spoon handle with gold gauze ribbon. Secure it at the top and bottom with a few stitches and trim the ends. Bind down the handle with cream satin ribbon, then repeat with gold, keeping the spirals even. Secure each ribbon with a few stitches.

2 Use a 30 cm/12 in length of cream ribbon to make a carrying loop and stitch to the top. Cover the raw ends with a wide cream ribbon. Tie a ribbon bow and stitch to the spoon just above the bowl, adding narrow ribbon streamers, flowers and a good luck charm.

For many centuries, ribbons have been used for both practical and decorative purposes. Nowadays, they can be used for everything from gift wrapping to home decoration. They come in a variety of sizes and materials and it's worth collecting beautiful inspiring ribbons for your ribbon box.

We've given you two simple, but effective, ideas for decorating with ribbons, but with a little imagination you can work your own magic, at remarkably little expense.

Christmas Tree Decorations

Bright multicoloured ribbon decorations make a change from traditional red and gold at Christmas. Add gold-covered chocolate coins to make flashy medals, twist organza ribbons into sumptuous roses, and finish ribbon rosettes with sparkling buttons.

YOU WILL NEED

● a selection of ribbons, including wide ribbons and narrow wire-edged ribbons
● scissors
● needle and thread
● gold coins or buttons
● gold cord or thread
● PVA (white) glue

1 Cut two equal lengths of wide ribbon and fold the ends in to the middle. Place the ribbon bows at right angles to each other and stitch the centres together.

2 Stitch together two loops of wire-edged ribbon in the same way and attach diagonally to the first cross. Add a coin or button to the centre. To make a hanging loop, cut a length of gold cord or thread for each decoration and stick in place.

RIBBONS is published by Lorenz Books, priced £6.95.

Ribbons
stylish, inspiring ideas

Can't We Be Friends?

It was one thing to hold out the hand of friendship to this young girl. Quite another to get her to accept it.

By Audrey E. Groom

"WHERE have you been, Anna — it's nearly one o'clock in the morning. Surely you knew I'd be worried." Eileen could have bitten back the words as soon as she'd said them, for her granddaughter's face was dark with anger.

Anna lifted her chin defiantly. "I've been at the disco — you knew where I was, Gran."

"Yes — but —" Eileen turned away, struggling not to explode into recrimination about the time. "I thought the disco was over at eleven," she said eventually.

"So it was." Anna's face wore an enigmatic look as she made for the stairs. "And I'm going to bed now."

Eileen watched the girl run up the stairs, her brown hair, excessively styled, looking a little forlorn now; a little tired.

And the long black sweatshirt, huge and shapeless, seemed to hang limply on her slim shoulders.

How Eileen longed to reach her, to make her smile, to feel some warmth between them again. They had been such friends when Anna had been a much younger girl.

Her daughter, Margaret, had suggested this visit.

"How about coming to stay, while Bill and I and the twins are away, Mum?" It had seemed like such a good idea. Margaret had a cat and a dog and was leaving her elder daughter, Anna, at home on her own for the first time.

This sort of thing had never been possible before because Eileen herself had worked since her husband, Charlie, died. But recently she had taken early retirement and had since found the days long and empty. So she'd really looked forward to a busy two weeks — looking after Anna, who had always been such an easy, friendly girl, and very special to Eileen since she was her very precious first grandchild.

How different everything had turned out to be!

Anna, just 17 and now at art college, seemed like a completely different person from the sunny girl of a few years ago.

Even allowing for the unpredictability of teenagers, Eileen was appalled at the gulf which seemed to have opened between them; appalled at the almost aloof disdain on Anna's face, the dark moodiness, and worse — the unhappiness which seemed to lurk in her once bright, smiling eyes.

OF course, this business of when Anna got in at night was a problem. Margaret had explained to her mother before she left, "Anna's usually in by midnight, and I'll tell her to try to stick to that while you're here."

Well — it was true. She'd only been an hour later than that tonight, but this was just the beginning of the fortnight. And how did one know at what point to really get worried?

Eileen tossed and turned in bed, not falling asleep as quickly as she would like to have done. But at least the next day was Saturday and Anna didn't have to be up early for college. That was one consolation and one less thing to worry about.

Eileen slept at last and awoke to the sun streaming between the curtains and realised it was already nearly nine o'clock. Slipping into her dressing-gown and slippers, she went down to the kitchen.

It was a wonder she hadn't woken before because the din as she approached the door was appalling.

There was a thick fog of smoke in the air, some raucous voice was yelling out a pop song from a radio and Anna, in a bra and pants, was lolling on a kitchen chair with her feet on the table.

Eileen literally pressed a hand to her mouth. The desire to say — get your feet off that table, at once — was so strong, that it was only with physical pressure that she held it back.

Something inside told her that that was exactly what Anna was both expecting and wanting her to say. But if she were ever to reach the real Anna, still there, beneath all this façade, she would have to be more diplomatic than that.

So instead, after a couple of deep breaths to calm herself down, Eileen said quietly, "What's all the smoke, Anna? Something burn?" She went across to the window and flung it open.

Anna gave an empty little laugh. "Mm," she said. "Toast." Then she re-buried her head in the magazine she was reading.

Eileen glanced around the kitchen. It had looked so neat last night. Now a couple of dirty milk bottles stood on the draining board, the sink was full of blackened crumbs where, presumably, Anna had scraped the toast.

There were jars of jam, marmalade and honey standing on the table, all without lids. And a couple of cups half filled with what looked like cold coffee.

Even the pedal bin was standing in the middle of the floor with two pieces of blackened bread lying on top, too burnt obviously even for scraping.

It was amazing, Eileen thought, that one person could create so much chaos, so quickly. And automatically she moved around the kitchen, tidying as she went.

Even then, she could feel Anna's eyes boring into her, disapproving.

"You do fuss, Gran," Anna said at last, and taking the offending feet from the table she stood up and went to make herself some more toast.

THE spiked-up tresses were all gone this morning, leaving a cloud of fine, brown hair with a pale, pretty but cross face beneath it.

She was a delicately slim girl, and, as she stood by the cooker with her long bare legs, Eileen knew Anna was silently inviting adverse comments on her limited clothing, too.

Remarks like 'Are you sure you're warm enough?' or 'Why don't you put a cardi on, dear?' would have been pounced on or laughed at right away.

So instead, with sudden inspiration Eileen said, "What pretty underwear, Anna — where did you get it?"

Anna shrugged and looked disappointed at being denied a battle but tried to stay casual.

"Oh! I don't know," she said. "From Mum, I suppose."

Eileen sat down at last with her bowl of cereal and coffee. Questions that she would like to ask ran through her mind but instead she asked, "Will you be in for lunch, Anna?" and received the unsatisfactory answer that she might be, but then again she might not.

Eileen allowed herself, this time, to say what was in her mind, "Well, it would be nice to know."

She was answered as she knew she would be.

"Oh! Well, all right, I won't be, then."

Anna bounced out of the kitchen and in half an hour called, "See you later," before the outside door shut behind her.

Eileen, watching from the front window, saw her march off up the road clad in skin-tight jeans and another enormous sweatshirt. But at least the hair hadn't been re-stiffened.

Anna came home for supper but there was nothing but a cold exchange of mundane phrases passing between them — an exchange that seemed worse than any row. Perhaps that's where she was going wrong. Perhaps she should risk the rows.

Yet she was half afraid rows might result in Anna flouncing out and not coming back at all.

SUNDAY presented her with yet another problem. A boy called round after lunch and Anna immediately indicated that they were going up to her bedroom to play records. Eileen walked the hall below, listening for sounds of music, noting the long, silent pauses and wishing she had thought to ask Margaret exactly what she did about these situations.

But when Anna and her visitor came downstairs, they were so casual as to be almost chilling.

"See you, Anna."

"Right — see you, Erik."

There was not even a touching of hands, let alone a kiss, as they parted at the front door, and Eileen shook her head, realising how little she understood this generation.

She remembered herself and Charlie — the tight handclasps, the stolen kisses, the blushes. How different everything was now.

"He's a good-looking lad," she said to Anna after he'd left.

Anna shrugged. "Oh! He's all right." Her eyes met Eileen's for a fleeting moment. "You don't think I fancy him or something, do you?"

"Well — I don't know, dear, do I? I thought, perhaps —"

"Well don't think, Gran." Anna's lips set in a firm line and for a moment Eileen thought her eyes looked suspiciously moist.

"You don't understand, Gran, so don't try to. Your life's all ordered and nice. Everything fits into a slot, just the way you want it. But don't imagine it's like that for everybody because it's not! Your generation are too sure of everything."

Her voice grew louder and louder as she spoke. Then she flounced off up the stairs and slammed her bedroom door behind her.

But this time Eileen felt she had to try to penetrate the silence. She went upstairs and knocked on Anna's door.

"Go away, Gran!"

Eileen tried the knob, but the door was locked.

"Oh! come on, Anna — let me in — let's talk, love."

"Go away, Gran!" came the answer again and, defeated, Eileen went back downstairs.

Really, she wasn't doing very well. Was it because she was too old to understand? Too out-of-touch to think of the right things to say?

She glanced at herself in the kitchen mirror, seeing the tired lines around her eyes and much more grey in her hair than she had ever noticed before.

An old woman — a tired old woman.

S HE was still feeling that way the next day as she walked around the supermarket. There wasn't much really that she needed to come out to buy, Margaret had left a well stocked cupboard, but Eileen felt perhaps she had been staying in too much.

Being in an unfamiliar supermarket, of course, things were difficult to find and she walked up and down countless wrong aisles before she found the simplest commodities.

Which is why she passed the hair preparations twice. And almost walked into the poster advertising them.

Are you feeling old and drab? the poster asked.

Have you lost your confidence? Make your hair shine with colour and re-vitalise your life.

Idly, Eileen picked up a package of the hair colour. She had never used such a thing. It wasn't for her. She almost replaced it on the shelf, and then thought, but why not? Really why not? She read on.

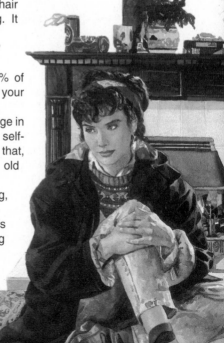

Semi-permanent hair colour. Covers 50% of grey, easy as a shampoo to apply. Brighten your life with Bright Colour.

On sudden impulse she slipped the package in among her other purchases, but covered it self-consciously with a packet of kitchen rolls, so that, at least, other shoppers wouldn't see an old woman's folly.

I'll use it when Anna goes out one evening, she thought.

But Anna seemed to go out less this second week, and was more unhappy-looking than ever.

So, it was under the cover of the blare of Anna's CDs, and in view of the fact that Anna's door was firmly shut, that Eileen took herself to the bathroom one evening to perform the great change.

She laid a big towel on the floor and another over the bath, washed her hair and then got out the magic tube and squeezed as directed.

She was happily lathering it in, when she caught a glimpse of her hands and nails. Goodness! They were brown too. They looked awful!

She sat on the edge of the bath. Perhaps she should stop before she made things any worse.

Then she noticed that she had dripped brown liquid over the towels, too.

In fact, she was just feeling most abysmal about the whole thing, when the bathroom door opened and Anna, package in hand, appeared.

"GRAN!" Her mouth dropped open. "What on earth are you doing?"

"I'm — er," Eileen gulped. "I'm colouring my hair."

Anna bit her lip and then let out a little giggle that she'd obviously tried to hold back.

"Gosh! Gran!" she said. "You're colouring the rest of you, too, aren't you? Look at your hands!"

"I know!"

"Oh, Gran — weren't there plastic gloves in the pack? Here." She picked up the discarded box. "See . . . you should have put these on."

"Oh!" Eileen felt small and silly.

"Never mind, Gran!" Anna said, putting her own box down. "Shall I finish it off for you?"

"Oh! Anna, would you?"

And, oh, how efficient she was. She put on the gloves and rubbed the colour in further, timed it by her watch, and then rinsed, and rinsed, until the water ran clear.

Eileen soon realised that Anna was quite enjoying herself, demonstrating her know-how in a subject in which her grandmother was a complete novice.

But that was fine by Eileen.

Anna was smiling — actually talking as she worked. And when the colouring was done, she quickly moved the stained towels, put them in a basin to soak, and showed Eileen how to get the colour off her hands. She even offered to blow-dry her hair for her, too.

"So, what about your hair, love?" Eileen asked when her own was all dry and shaped and amazing. She was remembering the package she had seen in Anna's hand.

Anna shrugged. "Oh! I'll do it later, Gran. I was going to use it because I felt so depressed." She smiled. "I don't feel quite so bad now," she admitted.

"Coffee, Gran?" Soon they were sitting at the kitchen table with mugs in front of them and their old companionship between them which made Eileen feel quite wonderful.

Dare she now ask the question which had been worrying her since she had arrived?

She chanced it.

WHY are you so unhappy, Anna?" she said softly. Anna shrugged and gave her a half smile and Eileen thought at first she wasn't going to reply. But then she looked up and said simply, "It's Don, Gran. He's got another girlfriend. I think it's quite serious and —"
She bit her lip and tears welled up in her eyes.

"Oh, love. I'm sorry." Eileen put her hand across the table to Anna's for a moment. "No use saying, 'there's lots more fish in the sea,' I suppose?"

Anna shook her head. "No," she said. "No use at all, Gran. Because he's special, and I still think about him all the time, I don't know what to do." She wiped her eyes with a hankie.

How tough these modern misses can be, Eileen thought, yet how vulnerable they still are.

"Well," she said, after a moment. "Times change, I know, Anna. My mother used to put on her stiff corsets when she was unhappy — so she told me. But you're going to colour your hair, aren't you? If it doesn't stun Don, at least he'll see you're not wilting away without him."

"Yes!" Anna looked up, eyes still damp. "I hadn't thought of that!"

"Well, maybe I can help you do yours," Eileen said. She stood up and looked across the kitchen to the mirror at her own dark, shining and shapely head.

"If you feel as different as I do when it's done — well — look out, world!"

Anna smiled. "What made you colour your hair, Gran? You don't usually, do you?"

Eileen shrugged. "Oh . . . I felt old and looked tired, and needed a bit of a boost, I suppose."

"You?" Anna was clearly surprised. "But you always seem so organised, Gran — so sure of yourself. I wouldn't have thought you needed things like hair colours to pep you up."

Eileen kissed her cheek lightly. "We all need things like that sometimes, Anna," she said and added, "and a little bit of luck, to make things come right."

And then she followed her granddaughter to the bathroom, where she helped her brighten her hair — and both of their lives. ∎

A Dog Called Lancelot

By Dorothy Ashley

PLEASE, Mum, say we can keep him." Five pairs of eyes were fixed hopefully on their mother's kindly face. But this morning, faced with the squirming bundle of fur that Jonathan, her eldest son, was holding on the end of a piece of rope, Mother was feeling far from kind.

Jane Hammond pegged the last of the washing on the line and picked up the empty linen basket. Turning a stern eye on all the hopeful faces, she said, "I've already told you, boys. We are not having a dog, and you are to take that animal back to Mr Whatsisname."

Jane felt most annoyed with the stranger who was trying to pass off his unwanted puppy on to her soft-hearted children. The boys looked downhearted as she began to walk back towards the kitchen, but Jonathan was not to be put off so easily.

Followed closely by his younger brothers, he hurried after his mother.

"Mr Watkins said if he can't find a home for Lancelot soon, he'll have to have him put down."

Ignoring Lancelot's brown eyes fixed on her imploringly, she turned to Jonathan.

"Emotional blackmail, Jonathan Hammond, will get you nowhere. I'm quite sure Mr Watkins will find someone to take him," she said, with an air of conviction she did not feel, and she went inside quickly before they noticed.

When Jane came back out again with another loaded basket of wet washing, the boys were still grouped round the dog, making a great fuss of

37

him and promises they could not possibly keep.

Lancelot was lapping it all up happily.

"Come along now," she said impatiently, "do as I say."

Jonathan turned pleading eyes to his mother. "Why can't we keep him, Mum?"

"Because I've enough to do with you five, that's why."

"We'll look after him, won't we?" And three eager voices loudly agreed with him. Joseph, the baby of the family at three, removed his thumb from his mouth and said solemnly, "I promise, too."

Jane sighed, put down the basket and placed her hands on her hips. She looked at each one of her beloved sons in exasperation.

"For how long — a week at the most? Then who'll be left to feed him, and take him out for his daily exercise? Old Muggins. No! And that's the end of the matter."

THE boys went into a huddle and started whispering. When their mother had pegged out the last bit of washing, Thomas, Jane's second son, tried his luck. Jonathan, the eldest at almost eleven years was, by mutual consent, the spokesman for his brothers, but nine-year-old Thomas was the one with the charm.

He now turned its full power on his mother. He had soft brown eyes and a dimpled smile and at this moment, in full pursuit of a family pet, the dimples were working overtime.

"We promise, Mummy, to take full responsibility for Lancelot. We have all sworn to take turns at looking after him, taking him out every day, even if it's thundering and lightning . . ." And everyone knew how scared Thomas was of thunder and lightning. ". . . And prepare his food. Cross our hearts."

"And hope to die," murmured the twins, Richard and Matthew.

Joseph wasn't going to be left out. Once again, he took his thumb out of his mouth long enough to say his piece. "Me, too."

Jane clapped her hands over her eyes, then slowly dropped her arms to her sides. She looked down at the five hopeful faces — six if she counted Lancelot — and shook her head.

She loved them all but she was determined to stand her ground.

"Listen to me, all of you. We are not going to take in a dog, now or any time, so stop wasting your time. And don't turn on the tap, Thomas — it won't do any good. Take that dog back — now!"

Knowing when they were beaten, the boys gloomily trailed across the lawn with Lancelot trotting beside them quite happily on the other end of the rope.

"You're not to take Joseph with you this time," Jane called out, "and close that gate. I don't want him running off again."

That evening when she told her husband all about Lancelot and her firm opposition to the boys' pleas for a dog, she quite expected him to say, "Quite right, dear, quite right."

But instead, to her amazement, she heard him say, "I don't see why the children shouldn't have a dog if they want one. It's good for children to have a pet. It'll teach them to be responsible and understanding. We always had a dog when I was a child."

"That was different," Jane snapped. "You were an only child. Your mother didn't have five boys to look after."

She wished immediately she hadn't said that because she knew Graham's mother would have loved more children. Graham, too, had told her before they were married that it was lonely being an only child. Well, she thought drily, none of his children could make that complaint.

The following day was Saturday and Jane was woken by her husband standing over her with a cup of tea in his hand.

"Mmm, I love Saturdays," she said sleepily and took the cup and saucer from him.

"The sun has got his hat on, so later we'll go out to play!" Graham laughed, adding, "The boys are up early this morning, except for Joseph — he's still fast asleep."

"That's unusual for them," Jane said pensively, but she forgot about it once she was up and preparing breakfast for them all.

Graham went off to the office for a couple of hours, promising to take them all wherever they liked when he got back.

"Have a confab while I'm out with the boys — I mean, have a confab with the boys while I'm out —" He thumped his forehead and Joseph, who was sitting at the table waiting for his breakfast, laughed with delight.

AFTER he had gone, Jane soon discovered why her sons had been so keen to get up that morning. She walked through the door in time to see Richard and Matthew, her seven-year-old twins, creep out of the back door with a dish of cornflakes and milk.

"Where are you two going with that?" she asked suspiciously.

Two guilty faces looked back at her and she knew instantly.

"You didn't take him back, did you?"

They shook their heads and Joseph got down from the table, milk running down his chin, and crept in between his brothers. "Lancelot's hungry," he said.

Lancelot was in the tool-shed at the bottom of the garden. Jonathan had just come back from taking him for his morning walk and, all unsuspecting, walked straight into the little scene in the kitchen.

He coloured when he saw his mother and only had to look at his brothers' faces to know what had happened.

"Immediately after breakfast, Jonathan," was all Jane had to say and he knew what she meant.

The boy turned on his heel and walked back down the garden. His brothers, without a backward glance at their mother, followed him.

Jane's legs wobbled like jelly as she climbed the stairs to make the beds.

Had she been too hard on them?

From her bedroom window she could see the boys having their last cuddle with Lancelot before Jonathan and Matthew took him away.

SHE finished the beds and had another look out of the window. Thomas and Richard were in high dudgeon, hunched up on the grass, looking for all the world like a couple of disgruntled gnomes. Despite the brief smile that flickered across her face, something was worrying Jane — but she couldn't put a finger on it. Something definitely wasn't quite right . . . Then suddenly it dawned on her . . . Joseph! He hadn't gone with Jonathan and Matthew and he wasn't with the boys in the garden.

She jumped up and rushed out into the garden and her flesh went clammy. The gate was swinging on its hinges.

She called out to Thomas and Richard, trying to sound calm. "Where's Joseph?"

They looked at her blankly and rose to their feet.

"Someone has left the gate open!" Jane cried.

Thomas said he and Richard would go to the park to see if Joseph had gone there. Jane ran out of the gate and down the alleyway running alongside their garden and met Jonathan and Matthew coming back without the dog.

Matthew was scuffling his feet listlessly as he walked beside his brother. Jonathan walked with his head held high but his lips were pressed firmly together to keep them from trembling.

Jane heard Matthew mutter, "I bet Mr Watkins'll be surprised when he comes back and finds Lancelot in the garden."

Jane's heart twisted at the sight of her sons' dejected faces but right now she was more concerned for the youngest member of her family. "Have you seen Joseph?" she gasped. "Someone left the gate open and he's gone."

Jonathan turned to his brother and said, "You go with Mum to the play-school in case he's forgotten it's Saturday."

Graham was home by the time they all met up again and there was still no sign of Joseph. "It's time we rang the police," he said and Jane nodded dumbly.

The boys huddled together on the sofa, whitefaced and miserable. Joseph had gone off before but he had never been away this long.

Their father picked up the phone and at that moment Richard cried out, "Here he comes — and look who's with him!"

They all crowded to the window and, with a whoop of joy, Jonathan leapt across the room and out through the front door with his brothers hard on his heels.

"Well, I never . . ." Jane murmured in disbelief.

Walking slowly up the path came Joseph, holding the hand of an elderly gentleman. "It's Mr Watkins, Mum," cried Jonathan, "and Lancelot."

MR WATKINS leaned heavily on the stick he held in his other hand and Lancelot trotted sedately beside him. They stopped in front of Graham and Jane, and Mr Watkins freed his hand from Joseph's clasp and held it out to Jane.

"Your son brought me here, Madam." He spoke with difficulty and had to clear his throat before he could go on.

"Joseph, he said his name was. I remember he came with the other boys." He nodded his head in the direction of Joseph's brothers.

"I've returned with young Joseph here because I want to thank you for your kindness in adopting Lancelot and I'm sorry he was ungrateful enough to run back to me.

"I found him in my front garden when I returned from the doctor's surgery. Joseph arrived just after I did.

"Please accept my apologies for Lancelot's bad behaviour. I'm sure he won't do it again. He's still a puppy, but I've trained him well: he's clean and obedient.

"I know he doesn't look much at the moment but, you see, I can't manage him any longer and I can't take him out for his regular exercise."

He patted the dog's head and went on, "He needs the company of young people, like your lovely family here." He smiled at the boys all clustered around Lancelot.

"You've saved Lancelot's life. He's the son of my spaniel, Arthur, who died last year. I'm going into a rest home next month and I was getting desperate.

"Thank you all."

He turned to go and Jane found her voice and pleaded with him to come inside and have a rest while she made them all some coffee.

Mr Watkins shook his head and thanked her. "I must get back. I have a lot to do."

The boys saw him to the gate and promised to come and visit him at the rest home. Then, with Lancelot sitting on the pavement beside them, whining softly, they watched him go until he was out of sight.

They came back to find their mother busying herself in the kitchen filling several mugs with coffee. Her cheeks were damp and she hastily rubbed them with the back of her hand.

"Mum . . .?"

She nodded. "Yes, Jonathan — but remember what you all promised . . ." The promise was renewed with hugs and kisses and lots of noise as they all rushed out into the garden with Lancelot, who had sensed the excitement and was barking furiously.

Graham crept into the kitchen and put his arms around his wife. "I suppose this means we'll have to go out and do some dog shopping?" he asked with a smile. "Leads and collars and dishes, that kind of thing."

Jane's answering laugh was a little shaky but as she laid her head against her husband's shoulder she knew she had made the right decision. ■

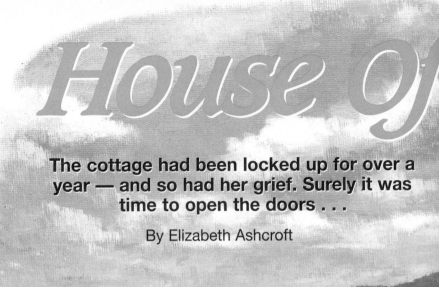

House Of

The cottage had been locked up for over a year — and so had her grief. Surely it was time to open the doors . . .

By Elizabeth Ashcroft

Memories

IT was a long drive. How many times had she driven this familiar way? She let her mind drift back over the years to remember Phil and Patsy squabbling in the back seat, surrounded by suitcases, buckets and spades.

Charlie the spaniel would be getting restless, his long, floppy ears twitching, his pink tongue licking her ear, slobbering, loving her.

Unexpectedly, at the memory of Charlie, her eyes filled with tears, and she blinked, brushing her cheek with a shaking hand, and hating herself.

Surely Charlie's death, so long ago, couldn't affect her more than Steve's? It was totally unthinkable, unreal. After all, Charlie had lived to a ripe old age, dying in his sleep.

At the time, they had all mourned him deeply and even now she still occasionally visited the apple tree at the end of the garden where they'd buried him. Steve, her beloved Steve, had died in a car accident, and she was still, after nearly a year, numb, and unable to give way to her grief . . .

Now, she glanced in the rear mirror at the back seat covered with bags. It was strange how she had an odd feeling she wasn't alone.

There was an almost-tangible presence in the car with her. She could almost feel Charlie's wet tongue on her ear, where he'd lean, wobbling towards her . . . hear Steve, saying impatiently, "Kate! Keep that dog away! He'll cause an accident! Kids, keep him back there with you!"

The narrow Cornish road, awash with sun and heat-haze, high hedges covered in wild pink and white flowers, was just so familiar. She could almost hear the excitement of the children, never still, unwrapping sweets, requesting stops, searching eagerly for the first glimpse of the sea through the familiar gap in the gently-dipping green hills.

"There it is! There's the sea! We're nearly there!"

43

Steve, capable hands on the wheel, would suddenly grin, as he cast off the responsibility of work, of the long drive, and getting the family there safely. Touching her knee gently, he'd say, "At last."

It was their personal bolt-hole, their haven. A small, sturdy grey cottage which had been Steven's father's. The end of a row, set back from a winding lane a mile from the village.

Outside, there was a riot of roses gone wild, and leaning trellis heavy with clematis. Inside, it was filled with, to Kate's eyes, beautiful things, for they all brought back a cherished memory.

The sagging old button-back sofa they'd rescued from a skip, the heavy velvet curtains bought at a village jumble sale. The simple pine table scrubbed and shining, which she'd spotted in a junk shop. The oddments of china, flower bedecked, even chipped, but chosen with love as presents from Steve and the children over the years.

Ahead, a lorry chugged along aggravatingly slowly, clinging to the centre of the road, so she couldn't pass even if she wanted to, the familiar narrow, curving roads making it impossible to see round the next bend.

For the first time, she wondered if she was doing the right thing.

"Go where?" Phil and Patsy had stared at her across the Sunday morning débris of the breakfast table. At Kate's feet, Sophy the cat leaned companionably against her bare legs, silver-grey coat warm, familiar. Kate could feel the whole of the small body quivering with happiness as she purred gently.

"The cottage," she had said tensely. "You're both going away, after all. I need to get away myself. To think."

"Think?" Patsy had echoed foolishly, and Kate had felt unaccustomed anger prick her. Was she so old, at 42, that she didn't need to be alone, to think? To Patsy, at 14, did she seem so utterly decrepit?

"Why not? After all, you're going to France with Mary's parents and Phil'll be back at college. Gran's looking after the house, and Horace and Sophy'll be company for her. It's all arranged, love. No more discussion!"

SHE'D known she wouldn't be able to bear the house without both of them. Without the constant shrilling of the telephone, the soon-to-be-forgotten arguments, the pounding stereo, the thud of feet on the stairs. She would be too alone, filled with too many memories. It had been bad enough when Phil had first gone away to college.

And how many memories will there be here, at the cottage, she asked herself, as her original optimism gave way to despair. You're a fool, Kate Drew. The cottage is Steve, us, the family. I'll be doubly alone there, staring at the sun terrace we began last summer, the painting half finished in the small bedroom with the eaves.

But I have to go, she told herself. I have to say goodbye. Just this once more.

For she'd put the cottage up for sale and hadn't yet dared to tell the children, knowing what their reaction would be. In a fury of decision she'd phoned her solicitor, an old and trusted friend.

"Kenneth, I want to sell the cottage. I never want to see it again."

"Kate!" He'd been aghast. "But you both always said you'd never sell it!"

"That was when we were together." Kate's throat was tight with still-unshed tears. "Sell it, Kenneth. Please."

He sensed her determination but still protested. "Think about it, Kate, and let me know."

"I mean it, Kenneth. I'll get someone else to do it if you won't."

As she put down the phone, she'd felt a great weight lift from her. She'd never see it again, the place where they'd spent their honeymoon, returned year after year, spurning holidays abroad, glorying in the rough Cornish weather, the wind, and the spray from the sea; the occasional glorious unforgettable hot summer of sand in everything, dripping cornets, all the windows and doors wide open to catch the errant breeze.

THEN, 10 days ago, she'd woken with a strange knowledge. She would have to go back. She couldn't let the cottage go without saying goodbye — almost as though it were a person, a friend. From that moment she was filled with a feverish purpose, phoning her mother, telling the children, forestalling all their protests.

She'd left them that morning, a trio of mournful, unhappy faces, bravely trying to smile. Phil had even come home for the weekend. Horace, the dog, had tried unsuccessfully to jump into the car.

"No, Horace!" Patsy had cried out crossly. "She doesn't want you! She wants to be alone." For the first time Kate had realised Patsy's sense of abandonment, lost without her mum.

"It's not that!" she wanted to cry out. "It's not that I don't still love you and Phil, don't still need you. It's just that somehow I have to remember Steve."

She'd been appalled to realise that during and after the agonising days of the funeral, she couldn't recall his face, his smile, his walk.

Even the photograph on her desk seemed that of a stranger. I must be a monster, she'd thought. Unable to remember my own husband, unable even to cry.

"Shock does that, dear," her mother had told her quietly. "It happened to me, when your father died."

But you had 40 years together, Kate had wanted to shout. We only had 18 — not even half a lifetime.

AGAIN, in the car, she had the sense of someone, something, accompanying her. She glanced in the mirror again and bit her lip. Imagination, she told herself, but a little uncontrollable shiver touched her.

Ahead, she saw the signpost to the short cut. Porth — and the rest was covered with clinging vine, swaying gently in the spring breeze.

Good job I know the way, she thought, and turned into the narrow leafy lane with a sigh of relief, filled with anticipation.

She found herself looking for the gap in the hills. Where was it, round the next corner, or the next? She slowed the car, searching the gaps in the abundant hedgerows, and there it was, as it had always been. The sea. A strip of silver blue, enticing, beckoning, as it had a hundred times.

"We're there!" she said aloud, gratefully, then glanced round at the empty car, feeling slightly foolish. "I'm here," she amended with reluctance. Had she made a mistake?

Maybe she should turn right round and go home again. It was only a little grey cottage, after all; had no life of its own. There were only ghosts there now; Steve's father, long dead, his brother, killed in the Falklands. And now Steve's ghost.

"Don't be stupid," she told herself, swallowing hard. She accelerated sharply and swerved as the car hit a pothole.

She fought with the steering wheel for a moment and brought it back under control. You are a grown woman, she thought sternly. You've come to pick up the bits and pieces you don't want to sell, and say goodbye to the neighbours.

She turned into the village street and the neat grey houses welcomed her.

The post office had been painted an inappropriate blue, and Miss Church at the Kettle Café had a new sunblind, blue with yellow flowers. Pretty.

And there was old Mrs Trent, with her fatter-than-ever corgi waddling along beside her. Turning, she recognised the car and Kate, and hesitated, not sure whether to greet her or not.

Kate wasn't ready to meet her just yet, and hear the familiar awkward condolences. She waved, mouthed through the window, "See you later!" and drove on.

Past the old schoolhouse, now turned into two elegant yuppie-owned cottages with, incongruously, swimming pools and double garages.

Foreigners, she snorted contemptuously, as they'd always snorted since the rebuilding began. Past the little Norman church, secure, safe, the tombstones leaning at angles, green with mould, but still with shining little jam jars of flowers placed randomly by the vicar's wife.

That's nice, thought Kate, smiling to herself. All these years dead, and still Mrs P. thinks of them.

Round the corner, up the lane — and there was The Cottage.

She caught her breath sharply, dismay and shock hitting her. Somehow, this wasn't what she'd expected.

A FOR SALE sign leaned drunkenly at the gate, its huge red letters shouting out to the world, "I'm not wanted!" She looked at the house as though she were a stranger, a buyer.

N O-ONE had been here for nearly two years and so it looked unloved, windows closed, a trellis hanging forlornly. Great clumps of pink poppies, seed scattered hopefully by Patsy the summer before last, straggled valiantly in the long grass, and one gutter hung despondently, the victim of a long-forgotten storm.

Oh, poor house. She got out, opened the gate, and drove in. She unlocked the door and lugged in her suitcase from the back seat, together with the plastic bags of food Patsy had urged on her.

"But the shop will be open," Kate had protested, while Patsy had stood determinedly clutching the bags to her adolescent chest. Then she'd even pushed the old wicker hamper on to the back seat.

"You might take longer to get there on your own. Or Mr Jenkins might have retired, and it's turned into a supermarket, open from nine to five."

"Heaven forbid!" she'd exclaimed, appalled at the thought. Then she caught Patsy, bags and all, in a bear hug. "Thanks, love. I'll phone when I get there. And write to me, both of you, when you go away."

S HE dumped the suitcase in the hall and breathed deeply. The familiar smell was still there — lavender polish, old furniture, the slightly musty scent so evocative of the cottage until the windows were flung open and the sea air whisked briskly through the house.

And there was a vase of flowers on the table, a plate with six round golden scones, covered by a piece of net, with a note from Mrs P., everyone's friend, who kept the spare key and an eye on things.

"Patsy phoned and told me you were coming. Welcome Home."

Her eyes filled with tears.

Oh, nice Mrs P. — everyone's guardian angel, both the living and the dead.

She stood in the tiny kitchen, remembering. The copper kettle Steve had bought at a boot sale, and spent hours bringing to a blinding shine . . . The rag rug they'd made between them one year, when he'd broken a leg. The small pile of tiles under the shelf where she kept her cookery books . . .

The tiles.

She went slowly over to them, a tidy heap on the wooden draining board. Thick Victorian tiles, all flowers and fruit and leaves, delicate Dutch tiles, blue and white. Oddments thrown out into skips, bought at the church jumble sale. They had sat in a drawer in the garage at home until Steve had had the brainwave.

"We'll take them down to the cottage!" he'd announced triumphantly, bringing them into the kitchen and dumping them on the table alongside her freshly-baked cakes.

"You're always grumbling about the sink at the cottage so we'll tile round it. Take them down next time we go, and if there's any wet weather I can put them up then."

"That's a marvellous idea, Steve. Let's!"

They'd tried them out on the day of their arrival, their last holiday, positioning them roughly, deciding where they'd go. She'd picked one up, seeing the price on the back, scrawled in pencil. "Ten and six we paid for this!" she'd exclaimed, aghast. "It must be worth a lot more now!"

"It's priceless." He'd taken it from her, and they both looked down at it. A thick white Victorian tile, with two shiny red-cheeked apples nestling among pink blossom leaves.

"Remembering where we got it?" he'd continued softly. "The market stall that year I lost my job, and you said we couldn't afford it. Then the very next day I got a job. Eureka! My lucky tile."

Steve had squared his shoulders, now free from the business suit and all the pressure that went with it. He'd always opened up at the cottage, become more carefree, younger.

"Right. The first wet day, and up they go. They'll be here long after we are, love," he'd added gently, kissing the tip of her nose. Steve, with his sense of history, of the past.

But that had been a summer of blue skies and warm breezes. Of hours spent in the sea, and sand in bedrooms from gritty, undried feet. Of the children brown and leggy, fast growing to adulthood, and not wanting to miss a moment of that special family closeness which comes when you know, fleetingly, that soon they will be getting on with their own lives.

They'd clung to each other, the four of them, beset by an odd need to enjoy that summer. And now she knew why — and was grateful for that last, long perfect holiday.

So the tiles were never put up. And now she fingered them gently, searching for the Victorian Apples. She felt the fine cracks in the still-shiny glaze, and welcomed its heaviness.

AND suddenly, the cottage was filled with Steve's presence. Steve, young and strong, carrying her with difficulty, and both of them giggling with laughter, up the narrow stairs on their honeymoon. Steve, serious, intent, with Phil, their first-born, bathing him in the kitchen on this very table. Steve, a little broader, helping Patsy trim the Christmas tree one year, unable to get the tree to straighten and giving up in the end, so all the ornaments leaned precariously to one side. The Crooked Christmas, they always called it jokingly afterwards.

Steve was all around her, and she stood in the small musty-smelling kitchen, held the Victorian Apples, and wept for the first time. And eventually she was filled with a strange aching peace as the tears streamed hotly down her cheeks.

Later on she went out to the car, remembering the other things Patsy had piled on the back seat. To her astonishment, she heard a plaintive meow from the old basket.

She opened it and hardly able to believe her eyes, there was Sophy, all grey haughtiness and ruffled dignity, as she climbed out and sprang nimbly to the ground. No wonder she'd sensed a presence in the car all the way to the cottage!

Smiling tremulously, she found the note tucked in the corner of the basket, Patsy's writing, sloping, still childish.

So you won't be lonely. Good job Sophy likes cars! Gran thought you'd like to have her. Love from Us.

She'd phone Patsy tonight, she thought, as Sophy walked round her feet, tail curling warmly round her legs. But first there was something she had to do.

Followed closely by the little grey cat, she walked resolutely over to the FOR SALE sign.

She took hold of it, tugging hard, and pulled it right out.

Kenneth was right. She could never, ever, sell the cottage.

There was too much of their past — and present — bound up in these four sturdy grey walls.

There was the shrill tinkle of a bicycle bell and she looked up, seeing Mrs P. riding unsteadily towards her on her familiar old bike, grey hair flying in the breeze.

She went to meet her gladly, knowing that, at last, she could talk about Steve. ■

A FAMILY

When a marriage ends, everyone knows you shouldn't take sides.
But sometimes, it's essential.

O H, Harry, she's sent it back!" Norma's dismayed voice carried from the hall to where her husband sat at the breakfast table. "Young Christopher's birthday present — Diane's sent it back, unopened!" Pushing back her curly hair, the middle-aged woman held out the parcel the postman had just given her.

"She . . . she says she'd rather we didn't try to keep in touch," she faltered, tears filling her eyes as she handed Harry the single sheet of notepaper. "The boy's settling down in his new life, and . . . and she doesn't want him to be reminded of the past!"

Harry frowned through his reading glasses at the neat, formal-looking letter. He thought of how proud Norma had been, parcelling up the watch that was to be their grandson's 10th birthday present. Sending it off, with a letter full of love and everyday news to the flat 50 miles away, where Diane and Christopher now lived.

"How could she do such a thing, Harry?" His wife's voice, unsteady with her pain, broke into his thoughts, and deep inside himself, he felt anger rise. "She . . . she knows how we've always doted on the lad, even when things weren't right between her and Steve."

Getting to his feet, Harry consolingly patted her arm. "Don't you worry about it, love," he said grimly.

Pulling on his coat, he pocketed both the unopened present and his daughter-in-law's cool letter. "I'll sort this lot out. See if I don't!"

"Now don't do anything hasty, Harry!" Norma's unheeded plea followed him out of the house.

As he walked, his tweed jacket flapping behind him, his eyes took in, almost automatically, the glory of late chrysanthemums which added riotous colour to the garden.

Christopher had helped him pot them in the greenhouse. Though neither of them had suspected, even for a moment, that he wouldn't be around to see them bloom.

*　*　*　*

"I'm sorry, Mum, Dad, but Diane and I have parted."

Harry's hand closed over the present in his pocket as he remembered Steve's pale but resigned face, that day nine months ago.

50

DIVIDED

By Carol Marsh

"We . . . we haven't been getting on for a long time, and she's decided to file for a divorce . . ."

"D-Divorce?" Norma had repeated the word with disbelief. "But surely it needn't come to that, Steve," she'd pleaded, her eyes suddenly darting fearfully to the framed photo of Christopher on the television set.

"You and Diane are just going through a rough patch, love — all couples have them . . ."

In answer, Steve had shaken his head, and Harry wondered, not for the first time, who this cold, seemingly almost emotionless son of theirs followed.

"It's all settled, I'm afraid, Mum, Dad," he'd said with a shrug and a sigh, as he looked from one to the other of them. "Diane moved out this morning, and took Chris with her."

*   *   *   *

It seemed like years since those words had been said.

Harry sighed now, as he turned into the factory complex that housed Steve's small firm. As always, pride and a kind of awe filled him as he saw how well his son had done.

Going round to the office, he knocked on the door, and went inside.

Steve stared at him in surprise from behind a desk full of papers.

"Dad!" he exclaimed. "What brings you here?"

In answer, Harry put his hand into his pocket and pulled out Diane's letter and Christopher's spurned present.

"Your mother's really upset, Steve," he said, as he watched his son's face darken with quick annoyance. "After all, the boy's still your son, and our grandson, and you know how much he's always meant to us . . ."

Steve sighed almost resignedly.

"I know how you both feel, Dad," he began, quickly, "but the thing is, Diane's made it pretty clear to me, too, that she wants to bring Chris up on her own now the divorce is going through. She's never considered me much of a father, you see, what with the business, and everything . . ."

At that moment, an adjoining door Harry hadn't noticed before opened and an attractive blonde woman of about Steve's own age entered the room.

"If you sign these letters, I'll catch the next post and . . ." Noticing Harry, she stopped, her eyes going questioningly across the desk.

"YOU haven't met Angela, have you, Dad?" Steve's voice, somewhat blustering in its attempt to appear normal, could not disguise the hang-dog expression which flitted across his handsome face. "Angela, this is my father."

As the young woman held out her hand, and he automatically shook it, Harry felt as if all the breath were being squeezed out of him. Suddenly, he knew, unmistakably, that the reason for the break-up of Steve and Diane's marriage was staring him in the face.

"Er, I'll have to be off, now." Mumbling an excuse, he made his way to the door.

52

At that moment, all he wanted was to put space between himself and his son — the spoilt, self-indulgent son he could now see cared for no-one but himself.

He walked slowly, as if much older than his 50 years, trying to work things out. In his day, people clung to their marriages: they were proud to be parents, and the joy Norma and he felt when Steve was born was something he would never forget.

How could their Steve, business or no business, Angela or no Angela, give up seeing his own child? How could he agree to Diane's new-fangled divorce terms without even the pretence of a fight?

HARRY'S anger and frustration grew as his fist tightened again around young Christopher's watch and the dismissive letter his mother had written. Almost without realising it, he walked around the corner and into the nearby railway station.

"A day return to Eastwick, please."

As he bought the ticket, he remembered grimly his promise to Norma to sort things out. Almost defiantly, he told himself he would re-deliver his grandson's present himself, and if Diane didn't like it — well, that would just be too bad.

Surely he and Norma had some rights, too, as grandparents? She couldn't just cut them off like this.

He boarded the waiting train deep in thought. As it pulled out, he half-closed his eyes, his thoughts clarifying almost in spite of himself. He realised painfully that his anger was still directed, not at Diane, but at Steve.

Try as he might, he couldn't forget that guilty look on his son's face when his secretary had come in.

He found himself remembering other times, both at school and since, when Steve had behaved less than honestly.

Harry sighed as he looked out through the train window, and a feeling of guilt washed over him.

Was he partly responsible for the way Steve had turned out: concerned only for his own, selfish pleasures, his business success that seemed to mean more than human beings to him? After all, Steve was his son — his and Norma's — and, as such, their responsibility. Perhaps they had just been too indulgent.

As the train pulled into the station, Harry got out, still deep in his troubled thoughts. He paused for a moment outside, and then asked directions. Soon he was hurrying towards the small school Christopher had mentioned in his few letters.

It wasn't far, and almost sooner than he anticipated, Harry found himself outside the neat, one-storey building. Instinctively standing under the shelter of a tree, he looked towards the playground.

It was deserted, and for a long moment, Harry wondered what to do. Then a bell suddenly rang, doors were opened, and a stream of children began to pour noisily out.

Harry caught his breath as he saw Christopher among them — busily engrossed in what appeared to be some swapping game with pocket treasures. He seemed totally at ease in his new environment, and suddenly remembering the words of Diane's letter again, Harry loosened his grip on the small precious parcel in his pocket.

His heart was swelling with pride as he saw how straight and tall his grandson had grown since the last time he'd seen him. His confidence and popularity were obvious.

But how could Harry approach him? Would he be foolishly reminding him of the past and all that had been lost; upsetting him in front of all his new friends?

Harry turned away, his shoulders bowed, and in that moment, he realised for the first time that he was not alone.

Diane stood there, looking paler and a little thinner than he remembered, a small lunchbox in her hand.

"Hello, Dad," she said almost inaudibly.

Embarrassment flooded over him, making his voice brusque, as he asked, "How long have you been here?"

Diane's suddenly gentle blue eyes met his. "Long enough," she replied. "You came to bring him his birthday present, didn't you?" she went on unsteadily. "I . . . I know it was wrong of me, sending it back like that, Dad. The last thing I should do is hurt you and Mum, but —"

"But you've been hurt so badly yourself," he finished the sentence for her.

As she stared at him in surprise, Harry lowered his eyes, the guilt and shame about Steve filling him again. "It's all right. I know the whole story now — or I can guess it. I met Angela this morning . . ."

"OH." Diane sighed. "I never really wanted you and Mum to find out," she admitted almost to herself. "Steve's always meant so much to you." As their eyes met again, he suddenly saw the depth of her loss and pain. The courage it had needed to come to a strange place and make a new start — a lone, rejected woman with a young child to care for.

As his gaze went back to Christopher, now energetically chasing someone, Diane said quietly, "He's missed you, you know — both of you — but perhaps you, especially, because of the way he used to help you, in the garden . . ."

Harry felt his eyes moistening. Trying to hide them, he looked away, and Diane went on wryly, "I'm only here because he forgot his lunch!"

"I — I'll be off then, if you've got to call him over," Harry said gruffly.

To his amazement, Diane held out the plastic lunchbox.

"Don't go," she said almost pleadingly. "You give him it . . . and . . . and his birthday present, if you like. He — he'll be so glad that you've come."

His heart almost bursting with relief and happiness, Harry took the lunchbox, put his hand into his pocket for the present, and, going quickly to the railings, called Christopher's name.

The boy stopped suddenly in his game and slowly turned, as if unable to believe his ears. A look of recognition and joy lit up his whole face.

"Grandad!" he shouted, and came running, as fast as his legs could carry him. ∎

Every Second Weekend

That was when Lucy went to visit her
father and her mother stayed at home
— pretending she didn't mind . . .

By Elizabeth Ashcroft

SUNDAY again. Lucy would soon be home from her weekend with her dad in his new flat.

Carrie looked at the clock. Ten to seven, with a hint of snow in the air. She'd just come back from a walk with William, the dog. He'd come rushing into the kitchen, hair standing on end with the cold, his long tail whisking round her legs like a breath of icy air, as relieved as she was to be back in the warm.

She bent to pat him. "She'll soon be home," she told him.

William was Lucy's dog, bought by Dave on her sixth birthday, and put into her arms one morning while she was still in bed: a small bundle of yellow fur with bright eyes, a lop-sided grin and a mind of his own, even then. He was Lucy's dog, and would answer to no-one else.

And now tomorrow was Lucy's 13th birthday.

Carrie sighed involuntarily

55

as she went to the cupboard and reached for the jar of coffee.

Funny how she always grew broody on Sundays, when Lucy visited Dave, even though the divorce, after tempestuous years of rows, bitter silences, and gradual distancing, had finally come as a relief.

Yet, after living apart from Dave for nearly three years, she missed him — his almost overpowering physical presence, his exuberance, his enthusiasm. Anything, from tennis to stencilling to renovating old furniture, he entered into with enormous abandon — then dropped after a couple of months.

The house had been littered with half-finished projects: cupboards which had been half-stripped and then hidden in the attic, the kitchen cupboards half stencilled, so that, with much nail-biting and ill-concealed fury, she'd had to finish them.

Mind you, it had done her good, and taken her mind off the loneliness, as she finished all his beginnings and then, to her surprise, started some new beginnings herself. She had enrolled at evening classes in car maintenance, and then began oil painting one afternoon a week.

And she had found herself a job.

She smiled, as she poured the boiling water into the mug, watched bubbles surface, smelled the steaming fragrance and wantonly, abandoning her diet, poured cream on to the whole lot.

She remembered Lucy's words one evening a few months ago. It had been Sunday again, and Dave had just dropped her at the gate, not coming in as he occasionally did. Another girlfriend, she'd assumed wryly — correctly — wondering why the thought should upset her.

"Dad doesn't believe it! He doesn't believe you've gone and got a job!" Lucy had announced, storming into the kitchen, giving her a bear hug, all legs and arms and skinniness.

Her jeans were rolled up as far as they would go, T-shirt all untucked round her middle, and hair a thatch of blonde tangles. Her wide blue eyes were enormous. Carrie delighted in her energy and unspoilt ways.

Yet she could have been so different, for Dave was always giving her treats, taking her out for expensive meals, in a belated attempt to make up for leaving her, the darling only daughter he idolised.

S HE doesn't need it!" Carrie protested one evening soon after the divorce. Lucy had staggered up the path with a huge teddy-bear.
"She doesn't need all these presents, Dave."
"She does. I enjoy giving them to her," he'd replied with dogged determination. "I miss her. And I'm missing seeing her grow up," he'd added, watching Lucy hug William and introduce him to the teddy-bear which was, incongruously, blue, with a plaid necktie. And much too young for a 10-year-old, she'd thought involuntarily.

"And whose fault is that?" she'd asked tartly, then bit her lip. She'd tried to keep their relationship friendly.

It was difficult, though, knowing he was missing all Lucy's "firsts": her first day at school, unfamiliar in grey skirt and white blouse, eyes serious with the enormity of a whole day away from home, on her own; her first walk into town on her own, with her best friend, Patsy, from next door; her first trip abroad, when Carrie had taken her on a package trip to Greece.

They'd swum in the unbelievably-blue sea, watched the fishermen come in with squid, and marvelled at the never-ending days of golden sunshine. Lucy had grown gipsy brown and more incredibly blue-eyed than ever, and her first boyfriend, an 11-year-old from Manchester, never left her side.

Lucy had labelled him soppy, out-swimming him, out-eating him, then sending him a card when she arrived home, signing it, Love, Lucy.

The wiles of femininity at 11, Carrie had thought, amused.

Now she sat down in the old rocking chair by the table and rocked gently back and forth, and William put his front paws on her lap and licked her face.

"Get down, silly," she said vaguely, sipping the coffee, remembering Dave's disbelief that she had actually found a job and that, moreover, she could hold it down.

She was working in a little antique shop in the arcade for four days a week, gradually learning the business, as well as making coffee and tea for old Mr Spinks, the owner.

He had arthritis and was going into hospital soon for a hip replacement operation. She knew he was worried about the shop with all its treasures he could hardly bear to sell.

She'd thought that perhaps it would be her chance to shine, to take charge, till a few days ago the old-fashioned bell had rung over the door and a stranger loomed into the shop.

She remembered how old Mr Spinks had hurried from a cubby-hole where he repaired china, restored bad paintings, and communed with his own familiar, a bright green budgerigar who lived in an old-fashioned brass birdcage in his office.

"He doesn't trust me," she thought out loud to William, who surveyed her in a sphinx-like manner and rumbled deep in his throat, green eyes filled with content.

Mr Spinks had been overjoyed

at seeing the stranger.

"Samuel! Samuel, my boy! Come along in, come along in!"

Samuel had come in, dwarfing the small shop, catching a small lyre-end table just in time as he knocked against it, grabbing a china ornament of a ballerina and clutching it in a big hand. He had grinned abashedly at her.

"Sorry. I always feel too big in Uncle Paul's shop."

SHE'D smiled weakly, taking the ballerina from his hand, and placing it carefully on the table. She caught his eyes on her, amused, and she blushed. Did she seem so old-maidish then, that he should laugh at her? Indignation welled, and she watched them depart to the cubby-hole curiously. She hadn't known Mr Spinks even had a nephew, much less one who looked like a rugby player.

Mr Spinks, after a short time, peered round the door.

"Could we have some coffee, Caroline? And some cream cakes, for all of us?" he added, pushing the boat out on this obviously great occasion.

Muttering crossly, she scrambled into her raincoat and ran across the road in the drizzle to the delicatessen.

This wasn't her job — she'd stopped being a gofer years ago, when she was 16, in her first job. She was supposed to be a P.A. here.

Then her sense of humour caught up with her as she drooled over the cream horns, the chocolate éclairs, the wickedly-tempting Danish pastries. She was lucky to have a job at all now that she wasn't exactly in the first flush of youth, much less grumble at having to buy cream cakes.

Back in the shop, she set an old rose-patterned teatray with delicate china, made coffee, and took it in to Mr Spinks.

LOVELY, lovely," the old man said jubilantly, his moustache wobbling with delight. "Samuel, this is my clever young assistant, Caroline. Caroline, this is my nephew, Samuel. He's in The Business." The Business, to Mr Spinks, was antiques.

Carrie looked at Samuel, realising that he was older than she'd at first thought. Maybe five years older than herself. Early forties, she hazarded, taking a great bite from her éclair and freezing in embarrassment as cream oozed over her chin. Stupid.

She wiped it off hurriedly, rose to go, and Mr Spinks spoke, muffled, through his Danish pastry.

"Samuel is coming in with us," he announced, and she turned, startled.

"He'll look after things while I'm in hospital. He's just sold his own business, and is looking for something else."

And, Carrie thought with an unwonted pang of anger, he wants to take over Uncle's business if he can.

Samuel was gazing at her serenely, and she flushed at the unfairness of her thoughts. Maybe she'd misjudged him.

But Samuel, as she soon discovered, was full of new ideas. He wanted to expand, to take over the small shop next door, increase their turnover.

58

"But Mr Spinks doesn't even want to sell half the things in this shop!" she'd protested one morning. "What's the point of expanding?"

"We can get in more furniture. There's more profit in furniture than bits and pieces of bric-à-brac."

He picked up the still-unsold ballerina and looked at her critically. "Once we start selling a couple of pieces of furniture a week we'll be in with a profit."

"You have to sell it first," she'd retorted, dusting furiously at a pine desk which didn't need dusting.

He'd been in the shop for 10 days now, and the whole atmosphere had changed. From being a cosy, dusty little bolthole with a few regular customers, it was now an unfamiliar, busy little organisation with all kinds of new methods and customers.

He'd even taken her out to an auction on Friday, to teach her the rudiments of bidding and spotting a bargain.

On the way home, his estate car laden with boxes of lace and old books and even a couple of rusty old wrought-iron pub tables, he'd asked her if she'd finish the day by having dinner with him.

Sitting at his side, bundled up in boots, a woolly hat and thick woolly scarf, she'd laughed incredulously. "Like this?"

"No." He surveyed her in the glare from oncoming cars as he stopped at traffic lights. "I'll take you home and you can change."

She remonstrated feebly. "Sorry, I can't. Lucy's home, and I have masses to do. And I visit my mother on Friday evenings — with Lucy," she added hastily.

"You do?" He looked at her quizzically, revved up the engine unnecessarily loudly before accelerating away as the lights changed.

"Uncle Paul is going into hospital next week, Carrie. So I'm afraid you're stuck with me and my methods for at least two months. Do you think you can stand it?"

"I have to." The words came out before she knew it, and she realised she had offended him. "I'm sorry! I didn't mean that! I just — need the job," she added lamely.

He pulled up outside the house. He was a good driver. He seemed to be good at everything. He was a finisher, not a dilettante, like Dave, and, for a split second, she resented it, and him.

He had no right to be so different to Dave, whom she'd loved, and married, whom she still kept supplied with home-made cakes and jam, delivered by Lucy.

"There's another auction next week," he announced, his good humour apparently restored. "I'll find out what time it is, and we'll go early to get there in time to have a good look round."

I won't, she thought crossly, getting out of the car, slipping on the frosty pavement. I won't do as he orders, just because he's taken over for a while.

But as she let herself into the house, and heard the car disappear, she felt oddly lonely, missing Lucy more than usual on her weekend visit to Dave.

NOW, she sat sipping the coffee, one eye on the clock. Lucy was late. Usually Dave had her home by 7.30 at the latest. A faint niggle of worry touched her. If she was going to be late, Lucy always phoned. She got up and went to the window.

It was snowing. Great fat white flakes slid past the window, flurrying, swirling, in the light slanting into the garden. William looked up worriedly, thinking he was about to be taken out again, and skulked behind the kitchen table. She turned, frowning.

Should she phone Dave, check that things were all right? But he'd only accuse her of fussing unnecessarily, and he was, whatever his other faults, a good father.

I wonder, she thought, what Dave has given Lucy for her birthday? Something outrageously expensive which I can't even match, I expect.

She thought of the delicate antique bangle she'd found in the shop, of the old lace shawl she'd bought at a boot sale.

Lucy at 13 was becoming clothes conscious at last, wearing incongruous mixtures of jeans and frilly blouses, borrowing her lipsticks and experimenting with wild spiky hairdos when she wasn't looking.

Maybe they're held up in the snow, she thought, idly finding another chocolate biscuit. But the worry prickled again. They are late.

How dare Dave let me worry like this! It's just as it was when we were married, she recalled. The times he forgot to tell me he'd be late, and I sat here in this same chair and worried till he came home safe and sound.

The clock on the old-fashioned dresser chimed loudly. Eight o'clock.

Oh, it was too bad. She should have gone out herself, she thought angrily. After all, Samuel had asked her out again on Saturday morning in the shop.

"Did you say Lucy is visiting her father this weekend?" He'd looked at her over a pile of old manuscripts he'd discovered hidden in a drawer.

There was a smudge of dust on his forehead and a cobweb hung from his hair. Suddenly, he looked oddly vulnerable and very attractive.

She nodded, wondering what was coming next.

"Sundays are good days for drives in the country. And a drink in a pub by the river, maybe?"

"In this weather?" She'd glanced out at the fog and the scurrying shoppers, their breath blowing like clouds in front of them.

For a fleeting moment she was tempted, but something held her back. She felt a strange reluctance to commit herself.

She hadn't even been out with another man since the divorce. Somehow, she couldn't imagine sitting next to a stranger in the theatre, or opposite him in a restaurant, indulging in the idle chatter of acquaintants. She felt oddly constrained, shy, at the thought.

"Sorry. I really can't."

He'd gone back to the manuscripts, disappointed, and although she'd wanted, momentarily, to change her mind, she resisted.

Of course, Dave had had three or four girlfriends since the divorce. Lucy had told her so, lightly, seemingly unconcerned, trying to hide her puzzlement and hurt.

"She came with us," she'd told Carrie the first time. "Came to the pictures and ate a whole box of chocolates. And her hair was out of a bottle," she added disdainfully. "You should have seen the roots — all brown."

But Lucy hadn't mentioned anyone lately and, in fact, now Carrie thought about it, she'd been strangely quiet after each visit.

There was the sound of a car pulling up outside, and she took a deep breath, forcing back the anger which threatened to spill over.

Lucy was back, that was the main thing. It wasn't her fault, anyway — she could only come home when Dave brought her.

THERE was a ring at the bell, and she went into the hall, wondering if Dave was with her, suddenly realising that she was in her old, well-loved woolly cardigan with the balled-up fur at the elbows, and comfortable slippers, furry moccasins with flat heels. Still, at least I'm warm, she told herself. Anyway, if Dave is there, he's seen me looking a lot worse than this.

She opened the door, braced to see him, but it was just Lucy who stood looking at her.

An oddly mature-looking Lucy, with serious blue eyes, and a thin layer of snow on her blonde hair.

Instead of launching herself on Carrie with a shriek of delight, she came into the hall demurely, carrying her overnight case in one hand, a parcel tucked under her arm, and a small posy of flowers in the other hand.

She thrust them at Carrie. "For you," she said, and Carrie took them, puzzled.

"From you?" she asked, and Lucy shook her head.

"From Dad. He says you'll remember."

A Victorian posy. Small, bright with colour, freesias and rosebuds, and greenery, delicate and sweet smelling.

Remember? Carrie looked down at the posy, and bit her lip.

He'd sent a posy like this to her the day after the divorce, with a note in his familiar scrawling writing.

To thank you for the good times, and Lucy. Now we both have to forget the past and look forward. You will always be my best girl.

Now, she stood in the hall, the snow swirling on to the carpet through the still-open door, and stared at Lucy. She looked serious, worried even, as she put down the bag and undid her coat. She had a pinched look about her mouth, a scared look in her eyes.

"Lucy? What's wrong?"

"Mummy . . ." For all her teenage maturity, she suddenly sounded like a little girl again. "Mummy, don't be cross, will you?"

"Cross? What about, love? What's happened?" she repeated, and Lucy's gentian-blue eyes filled with tears.

"Daddy's getting married again," she blurted out. "And he wants me to go to the wedding."

Carrie felt as though she'd been hit in the stomach, a sudden, stabbing pain, making her catch her breath. She put her nose into the posy and smelled the fragrance, and remembered his words. *You'll always be my best girl.*

The posy was a reminder now, as it had been then, of their good times past, which they could never lose. It asked approval, and earned a hope that she too would look to the future and make a new life for herself.

Suddenly, piercingly, she felt a strange sense of peace. She could start looking forward again. All this while, she realised she'd been marking time, while not knowing exactly what she was waiting for.

I'm free, she thought, looking down into Lucy's anxious face.

All this while, I've felt oddly responsible for Dave; even, she recalled with a little smile, doing his washing when Lucy brought it home at weekends, after his machine broke down.

Someone else can do his washing from now on. Oh, I'm so glad we stayed friends, after all the bitterness, she thought.

Then Lucy was giving her the familiar bear hug. "Mummy! You're not mad!"

"Did you really think I would be?"

"Upset. I thought you'd be upset. So did Daddy. He was worried. He drove around for ages, talking, worrying about it. Can I go to the wedding, Mummy? I've met her, she's nice."

Nice. Funny how the word didn't hurt as much as Carrie might have imagined it would. So that's why she's been so quiet after her visits.

Lucy was still speaking excitedly. "It's in April, in the spring. And Daddy's given me a coat for my birthday. A leather one — wait till you see it!"

Carrie held her daughter, feeling the young figure pressed against her, all angles and knobs still. Before she knew it Lucy would have grown up and moved away to start on a life of her own.

Samuel, she thought, over Lucy's flow of words. And she gave in to the surge of attraction that she had made herself reject before.

I will go to the auction with him on Saturday after all.

And to dinner, afterwards, if he asks me. ■

Follow That Cat!

Eight little bundles of mischief, yet none of them could replace the one I'd lost.

By
Teresa
Ashby

PUT down the telephone and turned to look at the expectant faces of my children. They knew — they had heard every word and there was no point trying to hide it from them. One look at my face told them everything. "It's Louis, isn't it?" Paul scrambled to his feet and ran over to me.

"He's dead, isn't he?" Samantha demanded, her face white.

63

Tears streamed down my face — how could I lie? How could I protect them from the brutal truth? I sank into a chair and heard over and over again that voice on the phone.

"You've lost a cat? I'm sorry, love, I may have some bad news for you . . ."

Over and over again.

Three weeks we'd been waiting, never giving up hope despite the fact that Louis had never strayed before in all his life — all 12 years of it. Every time I looked out into the garden, I expected to see him come stalking across the grass.

Louis was a ginger tom, but his mother had been a Siamese and this gave him delusions of grandeur. So we called him after the French king, Louis.

And for a cat as royal and proud as Louis to end his days under the wheels of a car . . . it was more than I could bear.

There were tears all round but at least for the children, the grief was soon cried out.

It was much harder for me. We had had him long before the children were born, and he was so much a part of us, always there, curled up under the table, or sitting on the window-sills at night, keeping watch.

It was when Tom and I sat alone in the evenings that it hit me hardest. For it was then that Louis would venture in and snuggle up for his regular cuddle. No children there to get in the way.

Everywhere I looked I could see him. Lying on a favourite stair, sitting under the table, hiding behind the curtain hoping I wouldn't catch him chewing bits off my plants . . .

Each time I came into the drive, I could almost see him squeezing himself under the gate to greet me — he was far too lazy to jump over the top and the gate always had a permanent rag of ginger fur stuck underneath it. In fact, it still did: I couldn't bring myself to remove it, and yet every time I saw it, my eyes filled with tears.

HE was still there, in my mind's eye, bright eyes always inquisitive and watchful, and it would hit me so hard . . . how could he die so suddenly, without any of the dignity he'd always had? Louis had a Siamese yowl. It always sounded so strange to hear it coming from a ginger cat. But he was convinced he was a pedigree, I'm sure of it. He had a small, pointed face and a lithe slim body and if he had wanted to, he could have been a skilled hunter who rarely killed, but brought his trophies home alive and unhurt.

How many times had I stumbled into the kitchen on a cold morning to find mice running around? Louis'd be sitting there among them, happy as Larry, as if to say, "Look, look what I've brought home for you — aren't you pleased?"

And I would have to dispose of them tactfully, mindful of his finer feelings.

One night, he'd dropped a tiny vole at my feet as I watched television.

"There you are," his expression had said. "A present for you."

The vole had looked up at me and I'd looked back at it in total astonishment.

I chased it all round the living-room, but it squeezed itself behind the unit, under the settee, and it took me two hours to catch it.

I'd placed it carefully outside and returned to the living-room, which looked as if a bomb had hit it. The furniture was all over the place — I'd even turned the carpet back in places.

Sitting in the middle of it all, glaring furiously at me for throwing his present away, sat Louis.

One night, two weeks after I'd heard the news, my husband awoke and found me crying, as was often the case.

"You ought to be over it by now," he said kindly, but he understood. He knew better than anyone else how special my little cat had been to me.

I was remembering the storm, the one they called the "Big Storm of '87." Our first thought when we got up on that horrible night, with the wind hammering all around us, was Louis.

We opened the door when the storm was at its height and he flew in, blown by the wind, his fur standing on end.

Seconds later, the wall beside which he'd been sheltering had crashed down, a pile of bricks and rubble.

"That's another life gone," we joked.

It was a joke because he usually kept out of trouble and we thought he had many lives left.

I had no idea he had used them all up.

M Y small son, with tears in his eyes, said he'd buy me another kitten and to my shame, I retorted angrily, "Another kitten? How could you? If one of you died, I wouldn't get another child to take your place."

My words upset him and I regretted them instantly, but it was true. The last thing I wanted in Louis' house was a kitten.

And anyway, why should I have another pet, and grow fond of it, only to have some motorist cut its life short?

Time heals, as they say, but Louis' memory was so sharp, so vivid, that I couldn't forget him.

Then, one night, my friend, Julia, knocked on my door.

"I'm sorry about Louis," she said simply. I invited her in and we chatted for a while, then she dropped her bombshell.

"I've come to ask a favour, Anne," she said, a little uncomfortably, I thought. "You know that my Tizzy is pregnant . . .?"

"No," I said firmly, before she could get any further. "I'm having no more cats. Absolutely not. I couldn't."

I'd given away his food, thrown out his dishes and his toys. It was the hardest thing I'd ever had to do.

"I'm not asking you to," she said. "I know how you feel. I wouldn't dream of suggesting that you replace Louis. But I do need to ask you a favour.

"I'm worried that Tizzy will have her kittens while I'm at work. Would you mind having her here until she's had them?"

Me? Nursemaid a pregnant cat? What on earth was Julia thinking of? I didn't know the first thing about whelping animals.

"I'm sorry," she apologised again. "It's a liberty, I know, but I wouldn't trust anyone except you."

"All right," I heard myself say. "All right, I'll look after her."

Besides, I told myself, it would provide a useful, not to mention educational, distraction for the children.

I WAS indifferent to Tizzy when she arrived. She was a pretty little tabby cat with emerald green eyes, and we had a mutual respect for each other — but that was as far as it went. We didn't have to like each other. She waddled around, her huge stomach wobbling from side to side, and I often wondered how many kittens she had in there.

Julia came in every night to see her — and through them I saw the closeness I missed with Louis.

Tizzy adored Julia and the feeling was mutual.

"I'll be glad when this is all over and she can come home," Julia said tearfully.

"So will she," I smiled.

The kittens were born one lunchtime. I daren't leave the cat and had to call the school to explain why my children would have to walk home alone.

They arrived, faces glowing, eyes bright, just as number four was being born. So far, all were alive, healthy and the same colour as Mum.

I needn't have worried about not knowing what to do. Tizzy was quite capable and I just hovered around in case she needed me. Seven kittens were born — wet, writhing bundles with eyes tightly shut, but she was still panting and it looked as if another was to come.

We held our breath, waiting; when it came, we all gasped.

Even my youngest went quiet.

Number eight, the last one, looked more ginger and much smaller than the others.

Tizzy did not like him at all, and I wondered if it was because he was weak or because he didn't look like any of the others.

"Oh, you horrible cat," I said as she pampered her other kittens, licking them dry. "How could you be so cruel?"

FOR days after that I had to endure the pleas of my children. "Can't we have him? Oh, please let us have him." It was out of the question. I had to stand firm on this. I was never going to be hurt again and that meant I would never love another animal again.

Julia eventually took mother and eight kittens home and once again we were without pets.

That night as I lay in bed, I realised I had hardly given Louis a thought and I felt instantly guilty. How could I forget him? I began to dwell on it all over again, but muscling in, demanding my attention, was that tiny ginger kitten, the one Tizzy didn't like.

"Thinking about Louis again?" Tom asked.

"No." I shook my head. "I'm worried about the little tom kitten."

Julia was worried, too. A couple of days later, she came round to see me. Wrapped warmly in the bottom of her bag was the ginger kitten.

"He's going to die," she told me. "Tizzy refuses to feed him at all now. She keeps pushing him away. She's taken a real dislike to him for some reason."

"You'll have to hand-feed him then," I said, refusing to look at him.

"How can I? I've only got a few days off and I can hardly take him to work and have him sitting beside my computer."

"All right," I sighed. "I'll take him for you, but he goes when the others go, OK?"

"Deal," she said.

I FED him with a dropper from an ear-drops bottle. He grew quickly once he was taking milk and was so different from Louis. Whereas Louis had been slim and elegant, this kitten was clumsy and ungainly and with a definite tendency to run to fat.

Rambo — it was my elder son's idea, not mine — grew so fast that I didn't notice when the time came for him to leave. He just stayed on. It would have been cruel to take him from Andrew, when the two of them had grown so close.

Rambo grew and grew until he was a mass of muscles and terrorised the other cats in the neighbourhood.

Well, of course I kept him — do you really think I'd ever let him go?

There was just one thing. I was tempted to keep him inside, a house cat, with a litter tray and glimpses of outside through a closed window.

If I'd done that with Louis, I was all too aware, he would never have been killed.

But Louis had had so much fun out there, catching mice, and chasing dogs — oh yes, he'd chase any dog off our garden, regardless of how big it was.

If I'd kept him inside, he could have lived on for years, but, oh, how bored and unhappy he would have been.

So I haven't replaced Louis — I could never do that. But Rambo does fill the empty space in my life and in my lap once the children are in bed and Tom and I are alone downstairs.

And when I see him, prowling around the garden, and chasing birds, I realise that it's the quality of life that's important and I'm determined that Rambo will have as much fun as Louis.

The King is dead — long live the King! ∎

Looking Fo

"GRANDMA . . . !" Lucy comes and sits in the armchair opposite me, curling her legs under her. At 13½ she's skinny, like I was, still shooting up, all boyish lines and angles. Yet, there is something about her face tonight which I can only describe as truly feminine.

Is it the touch of pink in her cheeks, or the luminous look in the eyes so like her grandfather's?

Her lashes are thick but short and I have laughingly commiserated with her about the fact that Robert and Andrew, her twin brothers, have long, curling dark ones.

When it comes to eyelashes, we agree, boys have all the luck!

We agree about a lot of things, Lucy and I.

Whenever I've come over to babysit, she's always — being six years older than her brothers — had a little time with me alone.

Then, she talks solemnly about things she feels her mother won't quite understand.

Now, I can see there's something else waiting to be confided, but she's having difficulty coming out with it.

"Grandma, I want to ask you something."

"Yes, Lucy?"

"About . . ."

In her bubbly personality, there's always been an endearing touch of shyness.

The curtain of brown hair falls across her face. With a flash of déjà-vu, I see myself at the mirror in the

he Right One

By Dorothy L. Garrard

bedroom I shared with Alma, my sister, back in Hammonds Green some 40-odd years ago.

"What about, dear?"

"Well, Gran, there's this boy, Nigel . . ."

I feel a fierce pang of protective jealousy and alarm. Oh, not yet!

It seems only yesterday she was still interested in dolls!

For goodness' sake, I scold myself fiercely, you're thinking like Eileen, her mother.

It's the very fact that you don't, which brings you all these precious confidences! I smile encouragingly. "Tell me about Nigel."

"Well, he's tall, with big shoulders because he swims a lot and he's good at sports.

"He's got black hair and greenish eyes and he's in the sixth form. He's seventeen.

"Grandma . . ."

Here it comes.

"Gran — how do you know when you're really in love? When it's the right one, I mean?"

The memory of a moment ago is nothing to the feeling I get now.

I can hear myself asking the same question — except that I was a little older and it wasn't my gran I was talking to . . .

I N Hammonds Green, I lived with Alma and my parents in a cottage in Candle Lane. I had won a scholarship to St Mary's College some 12 miles away and seemed to spend half my life travelling to and fro.

Attending St Mary's had cooled some of my earlier friendships a little.

Like Alma, my contemporaries had mostly left school at 14 and gone to work in local lingerie or footwear factories.

They now inhabited a different world. They had money to spend and were allowed to stay till the end, at dances. The rules, if not exactly abandoned, were relaxed, and their time out of work was their own.

I, on the other hand, had endless homework, and meagre pocket money.

I made casual friends at St Mary's, sometimes being asked back to tea.

Their houses were bigger and they ate food like junket and fancy cakes.

"When are you going to ask your friends back here, Abigail?" my mother often wanted to know.

In the end, it wasn't the worn linoleum, my mother's aprons or the faggots and tripe which stopped me.

It was the thought of my mother's hurt at their astonishment on finding we didn't even have a proper bathroom.

So I simply said that it was too far away for my friends to come.

She probably knew how much I wasn't saying, I realise now, but she accepted my decision and was perhaps secretly relieved.

All the same, she was worried about my solitude.

"Do you never see Josie these days?" Mother asked. She'd liked plump, jolly Josie.

"She's going out with a boy," I shrugged.

"At barely sixteen!" Mother registered automatic shock. She'd only just recovered from the horror of finding out about Alma's casual dates.

Alma was approaching 19 and seeing Alan Ferguson quite regularly.

Actually, I'd begun to get a bit worried about my own lack of male orientation, which my schoolmates seemed to find normal and absorbing.

THEY knew I was different to them in some ways and the teasing could have a slight, "How do they go about it in Hammonds Green then, Abby? Is there a village matchmaker?" I'd learned to flip back into the pond quickly when I was fished out of the water.

So I smiled, a knowing, mysterious smile which had worked miracles for the heroine of a particularly-awful "B" movie I'd seen recently, and intended to leave it at that.

But it had an effect I hadn't bargained for. There were drawn-in breaths all round.

"Oh, Abby! You've got a boy already, haven't you!" Norma cried.

"She's just said she's not interested in boys," Marie remarked, a disbeliever by nature. I responded defensively. "I'm not. He — he isn't a boy!" I blurted out.

"An older man!" they gasped, completely taken in. "Tell us, Abby — go on!"

"I don't kiss and tell," I fenced. That had been the name of the "B" movie. Surely, they must guess!

"Kiss!" they shrieked delightedly. "What's he like? Dark? Fair?"

A vague image sprang to mind and I'd already gone too far to extricate myself.

"Sort of . . . in between."

"Eyes?" They pressed.

"Huh . . . greenish brown," I muttered vaguely, wondering confusedly whose eyes I could visualise, mentally, gleaming at me, burning with passion.

Fortunately, the bell went for lessons and, being Friday, I hoped the heat would be off me by Monday.

They had such exciting weekends to discuss.

O N Saturday, Alma washed her hair then lounged around in her dressing-gown.

Where are you going?" I asked her.

"To the Palais."

"Who with?"

Instead of her usual lofty, "Mind your own business, child!" she said rather loudly, "Alan Ferguson."

Obviously, she'd decided to bring him out in the open.

Mother, however, filling the kettle at the kitchen tap, misheard and marched in.

"Adam Dyson! Alma Fulton — you will not —"

"Not Adam! As if I'd risk my reputation going out with him . . ."

Mother was so relieved that Alan got himself accepted with mere token caution.

What's wrong with Adam Dyson? I wanted to know.

I decided to wait and catch Alma in a communicative mood.

I lay awake that night, waiting for Alma to come home, thinking about boys and about Adam Dyson in particular.

Out for solitary walks, I'd come across him occasionally in the lanes. Once, he was leaning on a stile I wanted to cross, smoking a cigarette.

He was around 20, I guessed.

His eyes, surveying me with lazy curiosity, were a bright, greenish brown . . .

With a thump of the heart, I realised it was Adam I'd been unconsciously describing at St Mary's.

Scarcely had I made this discovery, before I heard the tip-tap of Alma's high heels on the path.

She tiptoed in.

"Was the dance nice, Alma?"

"Why aren't you asleep?"

"It's too hot."

"It's a wonderful night. I could have stayed out till morning."

The languorous note in her voice both intrigued and irritated me. Everybody seemed to know things I didn't.

"Did Alan kiss you?"

"Of course he did." She sounded pleased with herself.

"What was it like?"

"How can you tell anybody what a kiss is like?" she asked with affectionate impatience.

She hesitated, then came and stood over me. "Can you keep a secret, Abby?"

"Oh, yes!" I sat up eagerly.

"Alan and I have decided to get engaged."

"Didn't you tell Dad?"

"Not yet — Mum would get all upset if I told him first —"

"Alma. What's it like being in love?"

"That's another daft question. You'll know, when it happens. Now, go to sleep."

O NE Sunday afternoon a few weeks later, as I set off for another solitary walk to the old mill, my father called after me.

"Don't be late for tea. We've got company."

"Alan?" I asked, for, by now, Alma was wearing a ring.

"No, it's Mr Rogers," Dad yelled after me.

That surprised me. Luke Rogers had recently moved to a cottage on the edge of the village.

The grapevine said he was a writer and divorced which, I thought, would have been enough to give my parents reservations.

It was peaceful at the old mill.

I closed my eyes, smelling the grass, listening to a meadowlark singing his throat out somewhere in the deeps between earth and sun.

Then, sensing I wasn't alone any more, I opened my eyes.

"You're Alma Fulton's kid sister, aren't you?" Adam Dyson said without preamble.

"You're a long way from home."

"I came for a walk," I said shortly, annoyed by the "kid sister" remark.

"Done your homework?" He grinned.

Now, I wished I'd been wearing anything except my old skirt and a cast-off blouse of Alma's.

"Life's not all homework. What're you doing here yourself?" I retorted.

"Waiting for a girl, but she's stood me up."

He didn't sound very put out by that.

He fixed those narrowed eyes on me and the lift in my stomach went down, suddenly.

"Got a boyfriend, Abby?"

"Maybe."

Because I simply didn't know how to handle this encounter, I gave him that "B" movie smile.

I saw his eyes change. One of his eyebrows rose slightly. "How old are you, Abby?" he asked curiously.

"Nearly fifteen."

Actually, I was only a few months into 14.

As I spoke, the chimes of a church clock came faintly across the fields. I leapt to my feet.

"Where are you going?"

"I had to be home by four. Father'll be mad."

I'd forgotten the grown-up act now.

"I'll run you home on my crossbar."

"Oh, thanks, Adam."

He stood up and, before I realised he was going to touch me, tipped up my chin.

With a suddenness which shocked and thrilled me, I ached for him to kiss me.

But he didn't. Instead, he laughed, let me go suddenly and led the way to where his bike lay, behind the mill.

He held it steady while I inched on to the crossbar.

I was torn with terror all the way along the rutted lanes in case anyone I knew saw me.

Yet I also felt a sort of panicky excitement.

I dismounted under the huge oak, round a bend in the lane from home.

"See you when you've grown up, Abby," he called teasingly, as I fled up the lane.

LUKE ROGERS was already in the front room and I could hear Alma's voice as I whizzed through the hall. Mother came out of the kitchen with a laden tray.

"Why's Luke Rogers here?" I whispered.

"Something to do with his new book. He met your father in the pub and wants to talk to him about his work . . . smarten yourself up a bit."

Father was a cabinet maker.

For once, I didn't mind dressing up, thinking not of Luke Rogers, but of Adam Dyson.

To my surprise, there was pride in my father's voice when he introduced me. "Luke, this is Abigail. She won the scholarship to St Mary's.

"Now, she's doing a — um — commercial course, isn't that so, Abby?"

Help me out if I get stuck for the big words, his eyes pleaded with me and I felt a pang of love for him.

If this Luke Rogers put on airs . . .

But I knew, intuitively, he wouldn't, as soon as I met those grey eyes which were so clear, calm and honest and felt the firm, friendly handclasp.

The hand was square and felt very alive, like Luke himself.

"Hello, Abigail." I had a feeling he knew what I was thinking.

I frowned rather severely and went to sit on the remaining chair.

I ate hot scones and coconut cake rather absently while I listened and learned more than I'd ever known about my father's life and ways.

It was late evening before we realised it.

My father shook Luke's hand and, with a glance at Mother, for overt permission, invited Luke to come again.

"How old is Luke?" I asked my mother later.

"And why do you want to know his age?" She frowned.

"I thought he'd be quite old, but he isn't, is he?"

"I've no idea, Abby. People don't go around telling everyone their age."

"People always ask me mine!" I responded, and was sent to check my satchel for school next day.

DURING the following year, I hung around the mill a good deal but I only saw Adam in other places, in passing. He would give me that narrow-eyed salute which turned my stomach over. I was annoyed that I couldn't control the effect he had on me — like a jazz band in full swing, with my heart the drum and my emotional trumpets registering right off the scale.

Meanwhile, my acquaintance with Luke had developed into friendship, despite the difference in our ages.

One day, when I'd walked a long way, wondering if I might see Adam where the road from his village crosses the lane, I met Luke as I returned.

He was coming back from the village shops with a bag. "Hello, Abigail. Alone and palely loitering?"

Usually, I answered quotation with quotation, it was a kind of game. This time, caught out by the aptness of it, I blushed.

"Palely is entirely the wrong word, of course," he added easily. "I wish I could acquire a tan like yours."

"Ten minutes in the sun and I'm like a sunset with freckles."

I laughed, at ease again.

He went on, "Could you spare me a few minutes? I've had an idea. I don't know why I didn't think of it before. Come and have something to drink at the cottage."

The cottage was only one up, one down, with a kitchen and washroom built on.

The main feature of the living-room was an oak desk under the window, containing a typewriter and a litter of papers.

"Lemonade?"

"Yes, please."

I was smoothing the desk top admiringly when he returned. "I love this desk. Is it very old?"

"Yes. I brought it with me . . ." There was a sad note in his voice, as if they'd both been uprooted.

Then he smiled. "You're learning to type?"

"Yes, it's part of the course. I'm saving for a second-hand typewriter to practise on, but it's taking ages."

"I was thinking," Luke said slowly, sipping his own lemonade. "I'm snowed under by hand-written pages — I create that way.

"But they end up indecipherable with scribbles. Could we maybe come to some arrangement?

"I'd be happy to pay you to type out a readable copy, for revision. It would give you practice, too."

"I still make mistakes," I said, hardly able to believe my luck.

"That wouldn't matter, on a draft."

"Would I come here?"

"Your mother might prefer you to do it at home. I have an ancient portable you could borrow. And I've only the one room to work in.

"I could approach your parents for you, if you like?"

"Thanks," I said eagerly. I noticed his bookcase, another plain, beautifully-crafted piece of furniture.

My fingers itched to explore the volumes spilling out of it.

"Feel free to browse," Luke said, reading my mind. "I'll call by about half-past seven tonight then. All right?"

From then on I worked for him on and off. My typing improved no end and our friendship deepened. I even told him about my attraction to Adam. His only reaction was to look at me in a serious kind of way.

AT 16½, I left school and, the Saturday after I started work, I had another encounter with Adam.

Having surrendered a goodly part of my wages to my mother for board and lodging and obligatory post office savings, I'd gone into town.

I was determined to squander the rest on a bright, silky scarf, a lipstick and a knickerbocker glory in the ice-cream parlour.

I'd been a little too ambitious and was just scraping out my dish of strawberry and vanilla, when a shadow fell across my table.

"Hi, Abby."

Looking up then, I knew I'd just been marking time, waiting for today.

The jazz band inside me struck up, deafeningly, as Adam's eyes moved over me.

Adam sat down. "Fancy another ice-cream?"

The drums were so loud, I couldn't think. I shook my head.

"Coffee, then?"

"Why not?" I croaked.

"What are you doing now then, Abby?"

"Working for Meadows & Graham," I said casually.

I was eager to talk about the job I'd won, against stiff competition, but he didn't pursue it.

"You've changed." I smiled, that nervous, automatic "B" movie smile. His eyes told me how.

"Fancy a film? There's a good one at the Odeon."

"I've no money. I had a shopping spree," I said, without guile.

He grinned. "Playing hard to get? You're learning fast!"

Before I could react to that, he took my hand and I went with him, tingling all over, ending up in the back row of the stalls.

His fingers settled lightly in the nape of my neck. I'd no idea what the film was about, aware only of the punctuation of kisses.

When we emerged dusk had fallen. I made to turn to the bus station, but Adam, arm about my waist, tugged me in another direction.

"I've got the car."

It was an old, two-seater and extremely noisy. "Shall we go to Hammonds Wood?" he shouted above the engine.

"No!" I yelled back, scared stiff.

He frowned, then grinned. "Maybe next time?"

I didn't answer as I had a panic feeling of being in very deep water.

"Adam — stop here," I said quickly, as we sighted the oak.

Father could well be watching out for me, I realised.

Adam pulled off the road and turned me to face him. I saw at once he'd misunderstood.

"Abby — you're so lovely," he muttered, and pulled me to him.

I fought, fright turning to sudden terror.

When he did let me go, I half-fell out of the car, shaking all over and began stumbling up the lane.

"Thank you . . . for the coffee. And the film. I've got to go now," I squeaked.

Adam muttered

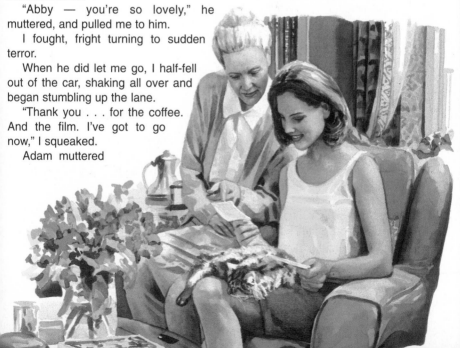

something I didn't catch, but I knew it was ugly, then he raised his voice, sarcastically, "You forgot your toys!" and my small packages dropped into the grass behind me. Instinctively, I stumbled towards Luke's cottage.

RAN into the cottage like a hunted deer. Luke got up, startled. "Abigail —?" With one glance, he seemed to comprehend more than I could ever find words for. His face was thunderous. He started for the door. "No — no!" I struggled for composure. "I'm all right. Really."

Then, suddenly, my legs wouldn't hold me.

Luke caught and held me while I howled like a baby.

When I fell into his chair, exhausted, he gave me a clean hankie and made me a cup of tea.

"D'you want to talk?" he asked, when I'd drunk my tea and splashed my face with cold water.

I didn't need to talk. I knew I had gone, armed only with innocent, romantic dreams, into an area where those things didn't count.

I just wanted to be sure I didn't do it again. I shook my head.

"But there's something I'd like to know, Luke. How do you tell, when it's real love?"

He looked at me with such rueful tenderness that my heart missed a beat.

While I'd regarded Luke as a fount of wisdom, I'd never thought of him in relation to other people other than my family.

Through him, I'd seen my father's good, honest worth, my mother's courageous battling with her own uncertainties and my sister's down-to-earth sense.

He'd illuminated my life in so many ways.

But what of his own?

"If only we could always tell, Abigail! The world would have a lot less problems.

"All I can tell you is, true love seems to me like a song inside — all harmony, no discords."

I blew my nose vigorously. "I heard a jazz band," I said dolefully. "So loud, I couldn't even think straight."

"Adam?" He guessed.

I nodded.

"I wouldn't say jazz bands don't come into their own, sometimes. It's a matter of wavelength — and timing.

"And, knowing you as I do, Abigail, I'd say both were wrong for you, right now.

"Put it down to experience, if you can. None of us grow up without a few painful ones, my dear."

With a few words, he had given me back my self-respect.

Forgetting about the divorce, I asked. "Have you ever been really in love, Luke?"

He hesitated. I couldn't fathom his expression. Then he opened a drawer in the desk and drew out a photograph.

The girl with a younger-looking Luke was dark and vivacious, with a prettily-pouting mouth.

"Jean was my wife. She preferred the jazz band!

"Yes. I loved her. But perhaps I was rather like you, Abigail. Of course, I was a bit older and knew a little more but it was still not enough."

He fell silent, slipping the photo back into the drawer.

After a moment, he said, "That was something I had to put down to experience. It was very painful. But all things work together.

"I recognised the real thing when it did come and I value it all the more."

A little shock wave ran through me. "You're going to get married again?"

Already, I had a feeling of loss. "I don't know, Abigail. Time will tell."

LUCY is chewing her lower lip wondering, I think, if she's been too daring. What can I tell her, except the simple truth? How can I explain to one who is so young? "Real, mutual love is a song inside you both, Lucy. One of you is playing the music, the other singing the tune.

"The music isn't complete without the singer, too."

She observes me thoughtfully with those clear, grey eyes.

But, perhaps, I'm not being practical enough. "I don't think it's possible to tell anyone, really," I add.

"But that's lovely, Gran. Like poetry. You sort of see between the lines. I think I know what you mean. Only . . ." she sighs ". . . I don't think Angela will."

"Angela?"

I feel a wave of amused relief. "She's really stuck on Nigel. To tell the truth, Gran, there's something about him I don't really . . .

"But, anyway, I'll try to talk to her," she says solemnly.

"Oh — hello, Grandad. Are the boys asleep?"

"Yes, Lucy."

Luke comes in and lays down the adventure story he's been reading to them. He smiles at me.

Time did tell, loud and clear. And the singing — and the music — never leave us. ■

The Badger

By Joyce Stranger

Inspired by an illustration by Mark Viney

Night is just a gleam away.
Streaked sunset clouds at end of day.
The woodlands now are hidden shades,
With creatures sheltering in the glades.
There beneath the hollow tree,
A wily badger comes to see.

He lifts his nose, he sniffs the breeze,
He lurks beneath the friendly trees.
No alien scent to give him fright.
He calls his mate into the night.
The young cubs follow, full of fun,
Play and wrestle, tug and run.

One paws a feather as it passes,
Another taps the seeding grasses.
Down to the stream the old boar ambles,
Leaves strands of fur on clutching brambles.
The sow is cleaning out her nest.
Bracken for the bed is best.

The old boar lifts his head. Now hark!
He's heard a distant lurcher bark.
Men's heavy shoes vibrate the ground.
He's well aware of every sound.
Back to the clearing now he races,
Into the sett his cubs he chases.

The men pass by. Their voices cease.
The badger family sleeps in peace.
Hiding now that day is bright.
Waiting for another night.

For Love Of Janie

One of us had to stay at home to raise our child, and though the task fell to me, I wasn't the one with the regrets.

By T. Ashby

YOU had your doubts about this and now, I confess, so did I. When they first handed our new-born baby to me, her little body squirming, her face waxy and screwed up, I felt as if a rock had settled in my stomach.

Her ear was crumpled, her nose squashed, and she looked nothing at all like those dreamy pictures in the books and magazines we'd been feeding our novice brains on for the last few long months.

But, oh, she was so beautiful with her sparse little crop of fair hair and those huge, knowing eyes.

She didn't cry, but lay like a lamb in my arms, and it was only when she began to blur before my eyes that I realised I was crying.

I could have sat there looking down at her for ever, marvelling at her pink, curled fingers.

I think I would have done, too, if the midwife hadn't scolded me with a business-like, "Come along now, there's more than one parent entitled to a cuddle."

Reluctantly, I gave her up and handed her to you, worried that you wouldn't see the beauty. But I needn't have.

I've never seen you look so happy, so pleased with yourself, so proud . . . or so near to tears. You held her close to you and that was when the doubts set in.

Five days later, we took her home together, and then the real fear began.

You watched me bath her; hovering, hands ready in case I dropped our precious child. You fussed and worried and I complained and fretted, sure

I would never get the hang of it.

Then came the day. You went back to work and I was left on my own all day, and no-one was more surprised than I was that I coped alone — although you never seemed to doubt my ability.

It seemed strange at first: me in my dressing-gown, feeding our little girl, you in your smart suit, rushing through your breakfast — when once we had shared the morning dash to work.

Our lives were so different now that I had traded the courtroom for the kitchen sink . . .

You still went to court and I could only sit enthralled and yes, a little jealous, as you related dramatic stories, which deep down I knew were largely exaggerated, to entertain me.

You'd talk of mutual friends and the grown-up world I missed. But I didn't miss my work, not really, for I was doing what I had chosen.

My life took on a kind of timeless quality in those days at home, measured in packets of disposable nappies. I swear Janie grew even as I watched. She didn't seem to be a baby long before she was up on her hands and knees, crawling around.

Each time I took her to the clinic, the scales gave a satisfying clunk as I laid her gently down.

JANIE had grown so perfect. Now, with her smooth apple cheeks and long dark eyelashes, she looked even better than the baby pictures I had once drooled over. Her arms and legs were chubby now and, as the health visitor pointed out, every crease, every line of her body, was perfectly symmetrical.

I often wondered if that was the real reason I was never accepted at the clinic. The chatting mums seemed to avoid my eye and conversation would become quieter when I walked into the room.

Somehow, I knew you would have handled it better than I did, but I was always aware that I didn't fit in.

When you came home tired, and Janie was ready for bed, I hadn't the heart to bore you with the mundane details of my day. Remember how you complained when I forgot to tell you that Janie had passed her nine-monthly check at the clinic?

You didn't know anything about babies, you insisted at the beginning. You said I was the natural parent, and I often wondered if the softness that came into your eyes when you held her was just a product of my own wishful thinking.

You seemed pleased when I did remember to update you on her progress, but sometimes I felt you were no more pleased it was Janie, than if it had been the child of one of your colleagues from work.

I know you offered to take a turn with the night feeds, but there was an agreement . . . my agreement! My rule — the one that said I was to be responsible for the baby and the house and you were to take care of the bread-winning.

Janie wasn't planned and threatened to turn our well-ordered, carefully-planned lives upside down — but when she came along, it didn't matter any more.

We must have been the most idiotically unprepared parents in history. Finding you're about to become a parent after 18 years of marriage was, I agree, a bit of a shock.

I'm sorry, but I began to doubt your love for Janie and yes, for me, too.

It was a dark area I suppose many parents must go through with a precious first child . . . that period of adjustment with so many new things to get used to. I didn't resent giving up my career because I'd never trust our child to a nanny, no matter how well qualified. I think if I resented anything at all, it was the sense of doing it all on my own.

THEN last night, for the first time in months, Janie woke and cried out. To my shame I didn't hear her and it was only when I found myself sleeping alone in our bed that I got up to investigate. The last place I expected to find you was in the nursery, but I followed the soft sound of your voice and that's where you were. Bathed in the warm glow of the night lamp, our daughter cuddled in your arms.

Instinct.

It was the one thing I couldn't learn.

You were singing . . . well, crooning, all those long-forgotten songs from childhood and gazing down at your girl with so much love.

I stayed where I was, hidden in the landing shadows, as you got up and laid Janie back in her cot. But you couldn't bear to leave her, could you? I returned to bed while you sat beside the cot, drinking in the lost delights of motherhood.

I wondered, had you done it before without my noticing? It was more than possible, for you two girls did seem to share something special, something that excluded me, a mere male.

I had lost nothing in this reversal of rôles and neither had Janie. That night I realised that despite all your brave statements to the contrary, the only loser was you.

You chose a career and now I know you've had second thoughts.

So this afternoon, I am going to see William to ask if there is any way that I may return to the chambers — part-time so that we may share, not only our working lives, but more importantly our daughter, too, because I'm also going to ask him if you can work part-time, opposite hours to me.

But only if you agree, of course, only if you agree.

And somehow I know you will, only too gladly. And this way, there won't have to be any losers, only winners, and we can all be together.

All three of us. ∎

A Love Beyond Price

She longed for her dreams to come true. What she didn't realise was that they already had . . .

By D.L. Garrard

THE building society right by the bus stop had given over its window to a display of local art. The window was always laid out attractively. Once there'd been a Three Bears' picnic, which had intrigued Sammy, and last month there'd been a Hallowe'en extravaganza.

Della and Sammy had plenty of time to look while waiting for the bus back from Ray's mother on Thursday afternoons.

Della's pregnancy with Sammy had been a shock, after a gap of 11 years, but it turned out to be the ideal tonic for Mrs Branson after the death of Ray's father. She simply adored Sammy, and Della had got into the habit of taking him over every week.

He was teething, and a bit fretful now he was away from his grandmother's fuss.

Della jiggled his push-chair rather wearily as she examined the pictures.

Abstracts left her cold, the few portraits were not particularly eye-catching, and pictures of

galleons plunging precariously into breakers were an uneasy reminder of the way she felt these days — pressured and slightly out of control.

The landscapes were more to her taste, especially the ones with trees. Trees attracted Della, with their impression of permanence and strength. She loved their way of bending before the wind, yet standing upright again when the storm was over.

Once, from a train, she had seen a line of trees on a hill, all permanently bent in one direction because of the prevailing wind. But they were still firmly rooted, refusing to give way.

Good for them, she thought, and discovered she had said it aloud when Ray burst into a surprised chuckle, and the twins and Julie had stared.

"Funny old Mum!" Patrick had said.

Phil had giggled and Julie, then nine, had been quite embarrassed. They were all practical, matter-of-fact, like Ray. They looked at her with his eyes — amused, affectionate.

Della had given up trying to share fanciful ideas with them.

She wondered wistfully if Sammy would grow up on her wavelength.

Now her eyes scanned the window interestedly — that painting in the corner!

It depicted a patch of woodland with the sunlight streaming through a leafy canopy of tall beeches, and the artist had caught the stillness of early morning.

The hint of lingering mist in the air heralding a fine day was so delicately real she could almost feel the freshness on her face.

For a timeless moment or two she was transported, then the arrival of the bus and the struggle to fold the push-chair and manoeuvre Sammy and her shopping, brought her well and truly back to the present.

AFTER Della had put Sammy to bed and gathered the rest of the family round the table for the evening meal, she mentioned the displays. "I don't see what any of them have got to do with a building society," Julie remarked.

Ray laughed. "Oh, there's method in their madness. I'll bet the Three Bears' cottage was in the background, wasn't it, Dell? Half-timbered, cosy, picturesque? They're saying you could have a country cottage, too, if you took out a mortgage with them."

"That's a bit far-fetched, surely!" Della said. "I didn't think of that for one minute!"

"You're just a Babe in the Wood!" Ray teased.

"It's called subliminal advertising," Patrick put in importantly.

"It makes you subconsciously notice and want things," Phil explained.

The twins' remarks always came in two halves.

"Any more sausages, Mum?" Phil went on.

"And for me?" Patrick added.

"Nothing subliminal about your wants — you're both bottomless pits!" Della sighed. "No. But there's some banana bread I made this morning, in the kitchen."

88

"We know!" they said, grinning.

"They've already eaten half of it," Julie observed, with the disdain of a slender 15-year-old.

"We can't live on yoghurt and a few grapes . . ."

"Of course, if you want to look like a dishmop on legs . . ." Patrick finished.

Della was glad she'd put the fruit pies in the freezer as soon as they'd cooled — she would have no time in the week to bake again. It was much cheaper using fruit from the small, narrow garden which Ray worked to full capacity. She had wondered if he would neglect it after he went to work for Peter Ainger, but he didn't.

*   *   *   *

Their marriage had presented them with Julie and the twins quite promptly. It wasn't until Della emerged from coping with small children, years later, that she realised Ray was barely tolerating his job behind a desk.

"Start looking round — after all, you spend most of your life at work," she encouraged him.

"There are a few ads in the paper I'm interested in," he admitted.

She worried secretly over several changes which didn't work, then the firm he was with closed down.

It was over a year before he found a job in a newly-opened market garden, Aingers Outdoors. The wages weren't high, but Ray's intense pleasure at finding his niche at last outweighed everything else.

"What's more, I can keep my hand in driving the Land-Rover," he added.

When their old banger had died on them, they'd been unable to afford a replacement.

"I've often thought it would be great to have a bigger garden," he went on wonderingly. "I just never thought of making it my bread-and-butter job."

Bread and butter, Della thought wryly, but not a scraping of jam.

Della eked out the pennies, but eventually she couldn't manage any longer. She declared her intention of temping.

She knew Ray wouldn't like that.

"I've always paid the bills!" he protested. "Anyway, how can you? There's Sammy."

"There's more to life than bills," she said with unusual firmness.

"I can get Sammy in with someone we see at the clinic, who's a baby-minder. Three short days a week — I'll still be home before you."

"But Julie will be off our hands soon —"

"Hairdressing isn't well paid, Ray. It's the love of her life — she's been torturing her dolls' hair since she was five — and if she wants to go full-time from her Saturday job, fine. But it has to be an apprenticeship, and she won't have much money for a while.

"And the twins are getting good reports. They'll most likely want higher education. Meanwhile they eat me into the red every week. It can't go on!

"I want to live a little now, not just at your expense. I'd love a real holiday, for instance, not just a day out."

"I'll look for a better job —" Ray began.

"No, you won't!" Della said crossly. "If you're not happy, then I couldn't be, no matter what I've got."

He sighed. "All right. If you really want to go out to work . . ."

She didn't, deep down. Rush and bustle flustered her. There were rapid decisions to make when there were hitches with the baby-minder, or Sammy wasn't well. Employers expected her to stay and finish rush jobs when her mind had already changed gear.

She tried not to let the pressure show. Of late, Ray had seemed uncharacteristically edgy. Was it because she was going against his wishes?

They'd always been in total agreement until now. But financially she could make ends meet for the first time in years without juggling, and what was more, she had started a savings account.

That could benefit them both. The holiday, perhaps?

THE following Thursday, the art display was still in the building society's window, but there were fewer pictures and they were rearranged. The woodland scene was now at the front, catching the real sunlight. Della thought how lovely it would look hanging in her living-room.

An elegantly-dressed woman paused to admire the pictures, and after a while, went inside. She emerged looking pleased with herself, and came to stand by Della in the bus queue.

"What luck I came past today," she said casually. "I've been thinking about a new picture ever since I redecorated my lounge. The colours in that one will go with it beautifully."

"Which picture?" Della asked politely, heart bumping, mouth suddenly dry.

She knew in that instant that she wanted her painting — "Morning Mist" — more than she'd ever wanted anything.

"The big one — the galleon. Quite good for an amateur, don't you think? Not that I bought it for its value."

Della scarcely heard for the wave of relief which swamped her. But, she thought, to be able to buy a picture costing £60 just because it matched your colour scheme!

While she was simply satisfied with making ends meet, some other person could come along and buy "Morning Mist," simply because it matched the carpet.

To her chagrin, her throat swelled with tears. You can't buy it, Della, she told herself. You've no money!

But I have! she thought. My savings!

"Do you think they'd take a deposit?" Della blurted out impulsively, quickly calculating how much she had in her purse.

The woman looked slightly surprised.

"For a picture? Oh, it isn't done that way. There's a spare telephone and a list of the artists' numbers, and you arrange a sale with the artists themselves. I happen to know the manager is friendly with someone from the art club, so it's two-way publicity, I suppose."

"Oh, I see," Della mumbled, feeling gauche.

But the bus turned the corner at that moment, and she daren't let it go because of feeding Sammy and preparing the evening meal for the rest of the family.

Her legs felt quite weak at the thought of what she'd almost done. She wouldn't begin to imagine what Ray would say if she walked in with a picture, a totally impractical object which had cost her £45. She'd talk to him about it first.

She found herself defensively cataloguing the things she had supplied for the family against all the odds. School journeys, bicycles, tap and ballet lessons for Julie when all her friends had the craze . . .

Wanting something for herself at last surely couldn't be called selfish, even if they didn't understand why.

"RAY," Della said, when they were alone that evening, "that art display is still there."

"Is it?" He turned the pages of his newspaper.

"There's one picture I particularly like. Just looking at it makes me feel happy and peaceful."

"Mm?" he said after a minute, when she paused.

There was a detachment in his manner which discouraged her. She changed tack and said lightly, "We've had no pictures on the walls since the children stopped bringing drawings home from school! Something colourful would look really good over there."

She nodded at the neutral expanse of wall above the settee.

"I'd have thought your cushions provided enough colour, Dell."

Della's cushion covers had started out as an economy, patchworks of odd material, then turned into a hobby. She had bought small remnants in vivid colours — cerise, violet, gold, jade — and edged and ruched and appliquéd them.

It had been an outlet, she realised now, the satisfying of a desire she hadn't recognised for something beyond the merely useful.

Suddenly, Ray got up. "Want the paper, Dell? I'm going to bed, I feel off-colour."

His good-night kiss was automatic.

Della bit her lip, disappointed, confused and a little worried.

Ray rarely had a day off work. He wore his good health like a badge of honour. When there was something wrong, her loving eyes noted it almost before he did. But she hadn't seen anything tonight.

Later she went softly upstairs to see if he wanted cocoa, but his eyes were closed and he didn't stir.

He wasn't asleep, though. Della knew that when she put out the light and lay beside him. He was too tense.

"Ray?" she whispered, slipping an arm across him, curling into his back. "Darling, won't you tell me what's the matter?"

FOR a moment Ray still didn't move, then he turned and pulled her close, as if he couldn't keep it to himself any longer. "The business is changing hands," he said, muffled against her hair. "The new owner — a Mr Freeman — had a place in Wibley, but the council bought the site as part of a development. He's bringing half a dozen of his employees with him and there are rumours that some of us will get the push."

The despair in his voice said it all — his previous bad luck, the work he loved being snatched out of his hands, and no prospect of anything else like it in the district.

"Is it just rumour?" Della asked. "Have you talked to Mr Ainger?"

"He's in hospital after a bad heart attack. His health is the reason for selling up."

"Can't you talk to the new owner?"

"We haven't seen him yet. It would sound as if I'm currying favour. The redundancies are hearsay, but it sounds logical."

Ray hated pushing himself forward.

"It may not happen. If it did, you could always go free-lance gardening. Plenty of people can't be bothered, these days," Della said into his unhappy silence.

"It's an idea — though I'd hate touting for custom."

She was relieved to hear the hint of a smile in Ray's voice.

"You're becoming as practical as I am, Della!" he teased.

No, she thought ruefully, just adaptable.

"How soon will you know, Ray?"

"Thursday afternoon, most likely. Don't say anything to Mum when you see her. She'll only worry."

*   *   *   *

The art display, which had taken a back seat in Della's mind, had vanished entirely when she passed the window again. She knew a pang of regret, but right now she was anxious to get home and hear Ray's news.

He was usually back in time to say goodnight to Sammy, but the baby fell asleep waiting, and she fed the twins and Julie because they wanted to get on with other things.

By the time he arrived she was strung up with worry, but it melted like snow in summer before the huge grin on his face.

"Oh, Dell — it's OK! Freeman's expanding! He's bringing better equipment, transport, everything! And I've not only got a raise, but use of the old Land-Rover at weekends as a perk. He said Peter Ainger had mentioned me specially!"

He swung her off her feet with a hug and a kiss, then gave her a flat package.

"And here's a present for you, to go on that wall."

Her heart jumped before she realised it couldn't be her painting. She hadn't got as far as telling him which and where, and in any case the parcel was too small and light.

Della gazed at the enlarged snap of Julie holding Sammy and the twins' cheeky faces grinning on either side of her. The original had been taken at Sammy's christening.

What could she say, except, "Ray, it's lovely. And what a beautiful frame."

"I asked Mum to get it for me, and I popped in after I'd collected the enlargement, to put them together. That's why I'm late."

He hung it, while she served their meal.

"We may not have much money, Dell, but what we do have is beyond price," he said, standing back to look.

He kissed her again before he sat down.

"Let's sneak off for a mystery trip at the weekend, when the kids are doing their own thing — just you and Sammy and me," he suggested.

"Shall I pack a flask of coffee and some sandwiches?"

"Why not!"

RAY drove into the country the following Saturday, through sleepy, winding lanes, and stopped in a lay-by alongside a wood. Della looked up at the tall trees and caught her breath in delight. "Ray, where are we?"

"Barton Beeches. A workmate told me about it. I thought you'd like it — you and your passion for trees!" he teased.

They had their coffee and sandwiches in the Land-Rover, parked in a pool of weak, November sunlight. Afterwards Ray lay back and closed his eyes with a sigh of contentment.

Della picked up Sammy and walked with him along a path covered in beech leaves.

She talked to him softly.

"Look, Sammy. This isn't paint on canvas. It's real, alive."

She laid a hand on a lichened trunk, feeling tranquillity, strength, all the things she couldn't explain to Ray, flow into her.

Sammy crooned, his gaze fixed on a slanting mote of sunlight just beyond his nose. He reached to grasp it, but a light breeze disturbed the leaves above. He watched it vanish and re-appear, dissolving into gurgles of laughter.

"What is it?" Ray called, alerted by the sound of Della joining in.

"Sammy's collecting a heartful of sunshine for me," she called joyously, not minding whether he understood or not, for they were still two halves of a whole.

"And you're right, Ray. We're fabulously, wonderfully rich!" ∎

TWO BY TWO!

Our colourful Noah's Ark cross stitch picture will make a delightful addition to any child's bedroom.

YOU WILL NEED

- 30 x 36 cm (12 x 14 in) white 22 count Hardanger
- tacking (basting) thread
- needle
- interlocking bar frame
- stranded cotton DMC white, 310, 444, 666, 702, 797, 970, 996
- tapestry needle
- 25 x 30 cm (10 x 12 in) mount board (backing board)
- strong thread
- picture frame

WORKING THE CROSS STITCH

Tack (baste) guidelines in both directions across the middle of the Hardanger. Work the cross stitch using three strands of cotton over two pairs of threads.

1 To make up: once complete, press on the reverse side. Stretch over the mount board (backing board) and fit into a frame of your choice.

Key To Chart

96

- 702
- 970
- 996
- 666
- 444
- 797
- 310
- ● Blanc

Back Stitch
- / 310

French Knots
- ● 310

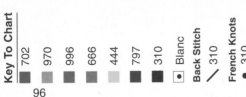

"I Like Your Style"

She'd always envied her cousin's big-city image. But would it work for a small-town girl?

By D. L. Garrard

G ILLY! It's been ages . . ." My cousin's attractive, husky voice laughed down the phone at me.

"Liz — how nice to hear from you again," I said with pleasure.

Things used to happen when Liz was around. I'd missed her when she'd left. We'd been friends, as well as relatives.

"How are you, Gilly?"

"Oh, you know me. My health is so rude it shouldn't be spoken of in public, to quote my brother, Jack!"

My emotions were another story, but I didn't feel like confiding in Liz just now. She'd make sympathetic noises and be staunchly on my side, but she wouldn't really understand — she never had that kind of problem.

It was Liz who called the tune and broke the hearts. Anyhow, she'd never met Barry, whom I'd met at a swimming gala. Swimming was the one thing at which I shone.

"And how are things with you, Liz?"

As if I needed to ask. Pretty, confident Elizabeth had been born surrounded by a protective bubble — with all the good things inside it.

She'd shaken the dust of Kirberton off her high heels some years back, and found a high-powered position in a large cosmetic company.

"Oh, life's hectic." She sighed, as if she didn't enjoy every minute of it. "What's new with you and the family? I suppose you're still with that health food place, what's it called?"

"Nuts and May!" I answered. "Yes, May's expanding and I'm in charge of the new Health Store. Brother Jack and Barbara have left the partnership and bought a vegetarian restaurant in the West Country."

"So Jack and Gill went up the hill, to fetch a pail of mineral water!" Liz warbled wittily. "Is that all you drink nowadays?"

"Not at all." I smiled. "I wouldn't turn up my nose at a sip of champagne and a taste of the high life."

"You could have more than a taste," Liz replied, enigmatically. "The truth is, Gill, I rang to ask you something. Could you possibly take a week's holiday at short notice? There's an exciting trip abroad in the offing."

As she told me the dates, I caught my breath. I should have been going abroad with Barry, but that had been cancelled. A week abroad with Liz would more than compensate.

Rome. Paris. Istanbul . . . Dancing under glittering chandeliers or tropical stars with handsome strangers who didn't demand more than I wanted to give, but whose gentlemanly flirting spread balm over my wounded ego . . .

"No problem at all," I breathed dizzily.

"Oh, marvellous! You see, Gilly, I'm in charge of a big cosmetic promotion in Brussels. I desperately need you to water my plants and look after my tropical fish and, most importantly, Suki."

"Suki?" I repeated, dazed by this sudden shake of the kaleidoscope.

"She's my pretty, aristocratic pusscat. I got her when I moved out of that

high-rise flat and I just couldn't dump her in a cattery so soon. Oh, Gilly, you're a darling!

"You'll adore my little cottage. It cost the earth, but it's worth it. Almost in the heart of town, but so tucked away you could imagine yourself in a village — cobblestones and everything . . .

"There's a park across the way, and shops and cinemas and theatres, so near, if you take the tube. Heaps of parties you can go to . . ."

"You're dazzling your simple country cousin," I said dryly. "Look, Liz —"

DEAREST Gilly, you've saved my life — oh, Suki — no! "Gill, I must go, Suki's after the fish. I'll collect you on the Saturday, about three . . . Suki —"

The phone went dead.

"What was that all about?" Mother enquired from the doorway.

I told her, and she exploded.

"Really, Gill! I used to get annoyed when you were fourteen and still at Liz's beck and call — but at twenty-four, to spend your annual holiday, cat and house sitting . . ."

"It's not like that. I'm fond of Liz, and . . . and besides, I didn't see it coming!" I protested irritably.

Mother had been worrying about my status quo since Barry's exit. I'd never had a serious romance before, and I'd actually believed he was "the one".

I soon guessed I wasn't his usual type by the ill-concealed surprise of his friends. He worshipped health and fitness, and small, vivacious women, but some things I couldn't alter, like being five feet eight inches, built to match, and basically a quiet, rather conventional person.

I'd been on a high at the gala, sparkling in the limelight, giving him a false impression.

He had invited me to make up a foursome at a villa in Greece. Sun-filled days and romantic nights . . . I'd agreed excitedly, but as our relationship progressed at break-neck speed, the thought of the nights began making me uneasy.

I'd tried to discuss the sleeping arrangements and the atmosphere dropped thirty degrees in as many seconds. I was made to feel like a stick-in-the-mud. I didn't know how to enjoy myself. When I'd had no choice but to cry off, my space was quickly filled by a pert, petite 18-year-old.

"We all love Liz, but she takes advantage," Mother was saying. "And I wish you'd stop running yourself down. You're no more a simple country girl than Liz — you were born in the same place!"

"But not with the same assets," I reminded her.

"There you go again! You should widen your horizons. There'll be no view from Liz's kitchen sink. Knowing her, the taps wouldn't be connected if coffee wasn't essential to her existence.

"Ring and say you've changed your mind."

"I can't, she didn't give me her new address. Anyway, it'll be a change."

"Well, don't you dare spend your holiday watching Liz's TV with her cat on your lap — in between spring cleaning for her!" Mother retorted.

That all-too-accurate vision stung me, where Mother's usual reproaches and admonitions didn't. After weeks of misery, I looked hard at myself and didn't care for what I saw.

A notion took shape in my mind, fed by Barry's remembered scorn; my mother's negative expectations; and also by my boss, May's, unsurprised reaction when she heard the Greek holiday was off — as if she'd doubted all along it would ever be a reality for me.

I made a decision. I'd use this chance as a springboard. Explore every avenue Liz had left open for me, go sightseeing, spend my holiday money recklessly, come back a New Me . . .

L IZ arrived in a zippy sports car, wearing white designer jeans and a sapphire top which matched her eyes. I'd put on the jump-suit I'd bought for Greece, because Barry like it. It was purple, pricey and not me, I realised now.

Liz's eyebrows went up approvingly, however.

"Hey, that's great, Gilly. Fashion comes to Kirberton High Street, at last!"

I slid into the low-slung car and strapped myself in before I disappeared below the dashboard.

The cottage was set in a quiet pocket between busy streets, and the small brick houses were painted white with glowing jewel doors. Steps with wrought-iron railings led up to Liz's crimson door and a flowering shrub in an oak tub repeated the colour.

"These were stables once, would you believe?" Liz said proudly.

She led me into the lounge, largely inhabited by greenery.

"Are you growing a jungle, Liz?" I asked. She laughed.

"I've pinned Suki's requirements to the cork board in the kitchen, along with everything else you need to know.

"Suki? Come and meet Gill . . . Suki? Oh, drat. She's squeezed through the window again and gone to the park.

"Knows it all, that cat — even used the subway," Liz went on, with the air of a proud parent. "Not to worry. She'll be back for tea."

"Suppose she isn't?" I enquired, alarmed.

"I'd like to see anyone try to stop her! Don't worry, she'll be here on time, making a din at the door."

She took me upstairs.

"Here's your room. Now feel absolutely free to use anything. Oh, and there are a few outfits in your closet — mistakes — mostly unworn. Have them if they're any use. Got to dash, I've cut it fine. Thanks again, Gilly."

She hugged me, grabbed two suitcases and vanished.

My room was small, but french doors opened onto a tiny balcony, from which I could hear traffic and distinguish the tree tops in the park.

I made a pot of tea and examined the cork board. It also bore a sheet of paper headed — GILLY'S SOCIAL ENGAGEMENTS. Someone called Adrian would collect me this evening to take me to a barbecue at Suzanne's.

This'll get you going! Liz had scribbled. You'll meet everybody, and get some more invitations. Adrian's available as escort, most evenings.

What did Adrian think about that, I wondered — and suppose I didn't like him? It doesn't matter, I reminded myself sternly. Consider Adrian the springboard for launching the new Gill.

I went to unpack. The clothes Liz had left were wide, long and loose, cousins to the fashion-wise purple suit. I tried on a burnt orange dress which must have drowned Liz, and padded into her room in search of a full-length mirror.

Freckles and a suntan didn't go with the image. I sat down at her dressing-table in search of a disguise. I was a bit like a weekend dabbler finding herself at large in a professional artist's studio.

I carried a palate of eyeshadows over to the window to assess the colours by daylight, and caught a movement outside.

Down by the crimson shrub sat a bewitching tabby kitten with orange eyes, watching a bee which buzzed about the blossoms.

I went to open the door. "Suki?"

She emitted a grumbly purr, then trotted towards the kitchen and the ready food-dish.

"I'm Gill," I said to her disappearing tail. "But not to worry. I've got things on my mind, too."

WHEN the doorbell rang a few minutes afterwards, I poked the mascara wand into my eye. Surely it wasn't Adrian already, for an afternoon cup of champagne?

With a hand over my smarting eye, I looked at the man on the doorstep. He wore a green checked shirt and light cords, and was substantially built, with pleasing, irregular features and doggy-brown eyes.

For the first time since Barry, I felt a twinge of interest in the opposite sex.

"I'd like my cat back, please," he said coolly.

"Your — er . . .?"

"Araminta de Sanguistina Merripole, pedigree Persian."

I'd have giggled, only his expression didn't encourage me. "She told me her name was Suki," I joked faintly.

"She'd stoop to anything for food. She's got a problem at present, she's on a special diet. My sister tells me you've fed her before. You shouldn't, you know. I can't imagine how she got out . . ."

"She squeezed through the kitchen window," I said confused, "but —"

At that moment, a seal point Siamese came sinuously up the steps, paused, ears pricked and paw suspended, while her sixth sense took over, then she flew like an arrow into the kitchen.

There was a blood-curdling yowl, a hissing and a spitting, and the tabby kitten tumbled across the floor head over heels in her hurry to reach sanctuary up the man's trouser legs.

He detached it with large, gentle hands.

"I'm sorry —" I stammered. "I thought . . ."

But I couldn't even hear myself. The Siamese — Suki of course — was still yowling.

"At least let me explain!" I shouted after the man, but a car opposite began revving its engine and the man kept walking, unhearing, to the end of the path.

I shut the door. The noise, boxed in, was unnerving. "Be quiet!" I yelled, stamping my foot. "That kitten's an aristocrat, too — and certainly a better mannered and prettier cat than you are in that temper! How was I to know?"

Amazingly, the noise ceased. Suki's mouth remained open for a minute, then she closed it and stared haughtily at me.

I went to get her dish, which had been almost emptied by Araminta. Suki ran past me, snapped up what was left, then turned to me indignantly, and began to yowl again.

"STOP it!" I threatened. I couldn't stand any more.

"Liz isn't here to spoil you, so be careful, your well-being depends on me!"

She eyed me with a modicum of respect. I had found the key to control, it seemed. Meet temper with an equal exhibition.

She gave me a sideways glance with her Oriental eyes, then tucked into her replenished dish.

I could see the shape of her bones through the sleek fur which rippled and shone. I supposed Liz had chosen her for elegance and superiority. Not a cat to comfort one, exactly.

Fortunately my need for comfort had taken a back seat. The encounter with the owner of the Persian kitten had roused my spirit, and the victory over Suki gratified me.

I washed my red and black eye, repaired the damage, fed the fish whose tank, I noticed, now had a protective cover, and realised it was past my own teatime. Before I could do anything about it, the bell rang again.

This had to be Adrian, if only by reason of the MG parked on the cobbles. He was slim, immaculate, lazy-eyed.

"Hello there, Gilly?"

"Hello there, Adrian?" The words sprang nonchalantly to my lips. It must have been the make-up and the dress talking.

"I'm early, I know. I thought we might go to the wine bar round the block and get acquainted over a drink first." He smiled.

"Fine. I'll get my bag."

BY the time I was settled in the dim bar, I could have murdered a three-course meal. I ate crisps and nuts, but the wine began to get the upper hand. Eventually, to my relief, Adrian glanced at his wristwatch. "We could be getting over to Suzanne's, if you like?"

"Fine." I stood up — carefully.

"Gilly —"

"Yes?"

"Suzanne's barbecues can be a bit messy. You know — greasy chicken, puddles of baked beans. Not to mention the pool . . ."

"Pool of what?" I asked vaguely.

He laughed.

"There's sometimes a bit of horsing around at the ornamental pond. I just thought you mightn't want to get that lovely frock spoiled. Silk, isn't it?"

"Back to the mews," I said. "Let's see if I can find a glamorous wet-suit."

I donned my purple suit, feeling if it got spoiled, it was one in the eye for Barry, and applied a different lipstick.

"OK?"

He smiled. "You're refreshingly easy to get on with, Gilly. Got a boyfriend back home?"

"Not right now. We had a parting of the ways. I hope Liz hasn't got some blackmail stranglehold on you, getting you to give up your time for me?"

"No. Judy — my girlfriend — is in Mexico. She's a courier. I don't get to see much of her, in season."

We set off in pleasant camaraderie, his hand at my wrist as he unlocked the car door giving me no qualms, though for some odd reason, I wished the Persian kitten man hadn't come out of his own door at that moment and observed us.

SUZANNE was a redhead with huge hooped earrings which would have made a tribal maiden envious. A glass of red wine was pushed into my hand and I was engulfed by the already animal crowd. Conversing above the taped music made me thirsty. I found I'd drunk my wine without intending to. Adrian came alongside. I grasped his arm.

"When will we be eating?"

"What?" he shouted, encircling my shoulders and bending an ear.

Across the crowded garden, my gaze met that of a man on the patio wall and I forgot what I'd been saying.

"Adrian — who's that man?"

"No idea. Amble over and get Suzanne to introduce you." He grinned.

"Not in this con . . . condition. It's just that I think — we've met," I explained, not very lucidly.

Eventually, the food was ready. I collected a blob of butter on one sleeve and somebody's baked beans in the folds of the other.

My paper plate seemed to have a life of its own. I made my way rather

unsteadily to the pool, with the fuzzy notion of washing my hands and splashing my hot brow.

I squeezed through the bodies and was just subsiding on to the rim of the pool when someone stepped backwards and bumped me. I toppled in with an almighty splash.

I shook the water out of my eyes and ears to the sound of laughter and clapping.

"It always happens!" someone was crying gleefully. Suzanne came running.

"Oh, why did it have to be you, Gill! Liz will throttle me for this!"

"S'all right. I can swim five miles, no problem." That innocent remark, from calf deep in the goldfish pool, brought howls of amusement.

I tried not to look at the Persian kitten man as I squelched past with Suzanne. Why couldn't he happen along when I was looking my best?

"Who is he?" I muttered to Suzanne, trying to be casual.

"Who? Oh, Anne Redmond's brother, Jeff. Anne's in hospital, been pretty sick, poor dear. Jeff called with a message from her. This really isn't his scene."

I took a shower and emerged in one of Suzanne's flying suits, covered in brass buttons.

Jeff Redmond had gone, and the way I looked, with my hair doing its own flying, I wasn't sorry.

ON Sunday, Adrian took me for a drive, and we met some people in the wine bar at night. During the week, when Adrian was in his executive suite or whatever, I tramped round all day sightseeing. On Thursday, I was fitting my key into the lock after a day tramping round museums, when I spied something up in the guttering.

It moved, and a pair of huge, distressed orange eyes peered into mine.

"Oh, no! You're not stuck!" I said in exasperation.

I ran upstairs and out on to my balcony, coaxing Araminta nearer. She came so far and no farther, and after a minute, I realised why. She was too afraid.

Quiet as the proverbial mouse, Suki crouched in the corner of my balcony, tail twitching, Oriental eyes gleaming.

Finally, I manoeuvred her through the french doors and shut them behind her. But I still couldn't reach Araminta, who was wailing like a vertigo sufferer at the top of the Eiffel Tower.

I removed my shoes, climbed gingerly on to the balcony rail near the wall, and reached carefully for Araminta.

My foot slipped. For a horrifying second, I saw myself smashing my brains out on the cobblestones. I grabbed for the guttering, missed, and toppled back into the potted shrub, which matched the one by the front door.

The commotion sent Araminta scooting over the rooftops. A voice from below yelled:

"What are you doing?"

"Playing acrobats!" I yelled back, furious with fright. Jeff Redmond had managed it again.

"Are you all right?"

"Stupid question!" I shouted. I hurt all over and I was near to tears. "Your kitten went over thataway, if you're interested!"

I tottered indoors. While I was in the bathroom, bathing my grazes and changing, the doorbell rang. I ignored it.

SUDDENLY I felt I'd had enough of everybody and everything, a surfeit of social life, sightseeing, and trying to live up to a false image. I lay on my bed and was asleep before I could count five recalcitrant kittens leaping over roofs.

The phone woke me.

"Gilly? Do you want to go to Barbara's tonight?"

"Actually no, Adrian. I've had a slight accident — nothing much, but I've been out all day again and don't feel like socialising."

"You sure? Only I've had a call from Judy. She's back home . . ."

"And you want to see her, of course. Truly, Adrian, don't worry about me. Nor tomorrow, I'll do my own thing. Then I'm off home, Saturday."

How sweet those words sounded, all of a sudden! Familiar routine, Chinese from the local takeaway, friends who liked the ordinary Gill and be blowed to people who didn't, including Barry, especially him!

"Thanks for everything, Adrian."

"Nice knowing you, Gilly."

I dragged an armchair in line with the TV. After a while, Suki sauntered over and indicated that she might condescend to sit in the lap I was making.

"Start kneading, and down you go!" I said brusquely.

We sat tolerating each other for a while, then I began absently stroking, and she forgetfully purring.

Next day I took a picnic lunch to the park. Suki insisted on showing me the way. She was accepting a bit of sardine from my sandwich when I saw a pair of light cords strolling by.

Jeff Redmond hesitated, then said uncertainly, "Er . . . Elizabeth . . ."

He was observing my comfy cotton trousers and T-shirt with some surprise. I shook my head.

"No. I'm Liz's cousin, Gill — in temporary residence."

"I see —" he said, as one receiving a revelation. "And — oh dear! I just took it for granted . . . Anne warned me to keep an eye on Elizabeth at number four, who was a bit naughty about feeding Araminta.

"But — you looked the part. It never occurred to me you might not be her. You seemed settled in, and this fellow kept calling for you . . ."

I registered his questioning tone with secret delight.

"Just an organised escort. His girl's back, now. I'm on my own."

He sat down beside me.

WAS worried about you yesterday, especially when you didn't answer the bell. I almost telephoned later, but you'd sounded so angry . . ."

"I was angry with myself. It's been an exhausting week, I'm not cut out for Liz's social whirl."

He smiled. "I didn't attempt to take over my sister's, except for Araminta — I was too worried about her, anyway. But the crisis is over now.

"We're twins, you see —" he went on "— very different, but very close, and we've no other family."

"I've lots of relatives but no brothers or sisters . . ." I offered him a sardine sandwich without thinking, so comfortable was his presence.

I took the last one, and Suki, seeing no more food in the offing, stretched and strolled away.

"Two's company . . ." Jeff quoted, and laughed.

I had a warm and lovely feeling that's just what it was going to be. ■

It'

By Suzanne
Thorpe

ll So Simple

Common sense told her the best way to get over one man was to find another. Unfortunately, her heart was finding it difficult to agree.

THE hall was cool, its languid shadows like fine chiffon scarves draped over the furniture, the sounds from the room beyond only muffled. Laurie would have liked to linger there. But the sitting-room door suddenly opened, releasing a cacophony of sound, and Gail rushed out to greet her.

"Ah, there you are! And I was just thinking you'd chickened out — well, come on then! Everyone's dying to meet you . . ."

Laurie took a deep, steadying breath and stepped into the room, where the party was in full swing.

It was like stepping on to a water-chute at a fun park, which careered in conflicting directions, carrying her senses on a giddy course. But this was supposed to be good for her.

At least, Gail and her mother both said it would be. What did they call it again — getting back into the social whirl? Picking up the pieces? Getting back into the driving seat after a collision of the broken-heart variety?

Yet, this was supposed to make up for Don? This crowded party, with its kaleidoscope of colourful clothes; with its 40 different voices; with its thrum of small talk and silly laughter; with its aroma of food and the scents of a variety of perfumes — this was good for her?

Funny, it didn't feel that good. Perhaps she could slip back into that cool, shadowed hall . . .

"Now, I'm not going to let you hide away." Gail's voice boomed and she steered a glass of chilled white wine into Laurie's recoiling hand.

"If I weren't married, of course, I'd never invite her, friend or not, she's much too pretty and I'd just hate the competition!" Gail said — and Laurie realised she was being talked about and not to.

Laurie gave her a warning look which went unheeded, then stole a glimpse of the stranger at her hostess's side.

He was tall, blond and smiling — Laurie couldn't possibly see what he was smiling about.

Her senses suddenly dulled. Instinct told her Gail was match-making.

Something inside her squirmed and panicked — Laurie wanted to grab

Gail's arm and plead: "Don't leave me alone with him!" But Gail had mysteriously slipped away.

SOMEHOW Laurie struggled through the next couple of hours. Martin, as the stranger introduced himself, was quite pleasant. His conversation was light and undemanding on her wavering attention. His looks were easy on her eyes, and his patience inexhaustible in coaxing each reluctant word from her.

Yet she found herself steeled against him. She knew her smile was tight and her eyes staring, as fragments of his conversation drifted by her like chaff on the wind.

Her mind was on Don. It was always on him, but seemed to focus more sharply when Martin's elbow brushed hers, or as their eyes met.

But she had tormented herself often enough over the last two months. Since the break-up with Don, she'd lost interest in everything around her, locking herself into her own little world of misery and heartache, where tomorrow always seemed another universe away.

She found herself brought sharply back to the present, when Martin placed his hand on her shoulder. She seemed so tired, he told her, could he perhaps give her a lift home? Throughout the journey she sat uncomfortably alone with him, in the confined territory of his car, and when he reached over to assist in unlocking the door, an alarm bell trilled off inside her as his hand skimmed over hers.

"I've really enjoyed our chat!" he told her. "Can we do it again sometime?"

But she was already out of the car, with a quite undignified flash of her legs.

"I don't know your number," he called after her as she dashed up to her front door.

"Are you in the book? Can I ring you?" he called. But she was inside now, and the door closed behind her.

YOU did what? " Gail gasped, having heard full well Laurie's embarrassed account of the meeting. On reflection, Laurie knew she had over-reacted, but she still resented the way Gail chortled gleefully into her delicious prawn cocktail.

"Look, when I asked you to join me for lunch — my self-esteem wasn't on the menu!" Laurie said indignantly.

"You're right!" Gail said, trying to compose herself. One last little giggle escaped and then she sobered into the stout best friend she was.

For, although they were the same age, Gail's bustling manner, her down-to-earth approach and her plumpness all made her seem more of a big sister than a friend.

"You asked me to lunch to make your mind up for you," she said, not pulling any punches. "But you've got to decide, and it's time you did, once and for all!"

"Decide what?" Laurie asked peevishly.

Gail answered her with a chin lowered, "don't-give-me-that" look.

Laurie did know what she meant. She had to decide, how had Gail put it,

"Either to keep on wallowing in self-pity, or have the courage to let go of Don and the past."

Well, that was an easy lesson to preach, but certainly not so easy to practise.

For the more she tried to convince herself she and Don were over, that she had been right to end things — the more she wanted to run from any semblance of life without him.

Her flat held no comfort. It felt so empty now.

The sofa they had so often curled up on now looked smooth and uninviting. The phone that had so often united them on his frequent trips abroad was now just an inconvenient intrusion from concerned friends or wrong numbers.

All those things only served to remind her of that last dreadful evening together . . .

* * * *

"I won't ease your conscience, Don!" she shouted.

Now, looking back, she couldn't understand why she had exploded like that. She couldn't erase either the memory of his face — or of the shock and hurt distorting it.

"Ease my conscience?" His words frequently returned to taunt her.

"I want to marry you!"

"So you won't feel so bad each time you jet-set off to the other side of the world?"

"What's got into you? You know my work takes me abroad — but there's nothing jet-setting about spending long hours haggling contracts over turbo engines!"

But her doubts had already turned ugly and all-consuming.

Part of her knew it wasn't Don she was blaming, but her own father and all of his years working abroad.

But another part

111

was too stubborn — too afraid to give Don that chance, the chance to make things work better than her father and mother's marriage.

*   *   *   *

"You're right," Laurie said reluctantly, coming back to the cup of coffee she was stirring.

"I never said a word," Gail replied.

"You don't have to! Besides, you've said enough already, over the past two months."

"So is it on, then?" Gail urged excitedly.

"Is what on?"

"A date with Martin Dexter, of course! He's thirty-two and dishy. He works in a bank — so you won't have to worry about him jetting off somewhere, and he's very healthy and outdoorish — loves golf.

"Now that would put some colour back in your cheeks!"

Did she mean Martin Dexter — or the golf? Whatever — it didn't matter to Laurie. She wouldn't really be on a date with Martin Dexter, she would be on a training course for the future . . .

Over the next fortnight she went on four such "training courses", and although Martin sensed her reluctance to take things beyond friendship, they got on well enough. He was easy to be with, and quite the opposite of Don.

Where Don was dynamic and assertive — planning dinner, or buying theatre tickets —

Martin was content to let the evening drift.

Where Don would have been outgoing and willing to meet new people, Martin would rather be in places he knew or frequented often.

So he had to be the perfect contrast — the ideal distraction from the past. Instead, Laurie found herself thinking more and more often of Don, and missing him more than ever . . .

"Y OU'RE in a bit of a state," Gail said. "I'm glad I popped round."

"Oh, I'm all right," Laurie excused limply. Gail's brows raised in question.

"Do you normally shred paper hankies like that? And has your hair seen a comb today?" Gail teased.

"Thanks . . ."

"Don't mention it — that's what friends are for!"

"Look, you know why I finished with Don —" Laurie began.

"Do I? I don't see how I can. Neither you nor Don seems to know why."

"My father . . ." she said, as if she were probing her way in the dark. "He went abroad five or six times a year."

"Like Don," Gail added, beginning to understand.

There was a long silence.

"Well, those years stuck with me. My mother ran that house while he was away. She rode every crisis, handled every decision — practically brought the four of us up single-handed!"

Laurie recalled the times at school pantomimes or prize-givings when her mother would sit there — alone.

"Yes?" Gail's voice was gentle.

"Well, my father would come home — the sun-tanned hero, his arms clutching loads of presents, while my poor old mum . . ." Her voice tailed off, unsure herself how she felt about it.

"There's just one thing," Gail said. "Does your mum know she's a poor old thing? I see her quite often in town and she looks quite a vibrant little lady. She seems to get more pleasure out of her memories than you do."

Laurie puffed out her cheeks in exasperation. "Thanks — what are you trying to do — shred me like these hankies?"

"I'm trying," Gail said, in the sort of tone she would use to a tiresome child, "to jolt you out of the limbo you're in! You owe it to yourself — and to Don — to let go once and for all, or admit you were wrong . . ."

Laurie had quite deliberately ignored the latter alternative.

"But it would have meant years of his working away. I was right to end it, I just know I was . . ." she said, in an effort to finally convince herself.

"And now it means years of Martin Dexters," Gail said meaningfully.

A heavy silence enveloped them as Laurie thought of Martin Dexter, or men like him duplicated over the years like a string of paper cut-outs.

"Ring Don," Gail said — suddenly and flatly.

Laurie's eyes widened in shock, then filled with sheer dread.

"Oh, I couldn't! I just couldn't!"

LAURIE didn't go out that night. Martin called, sounding very uncomfortable . . .

"I feel really bad about this, but my boss has squeezed me into a management training course up north. I know it's very last minute, but I'll only be away about three weeks . . . or maybe four . . ."

There was silence in Laurie's flat after Martin rang off, and then it was filled with a sound that had been missing for weeks . . . the sound of Laurie's laughter.

*　　*　　*　　*

Her decision to phone her mother with an invitation to dinner wasn't entirely an unselfish one.

"I've never asked you about Dad," she broached, once the gossip had been caught up on.

"How did you cope?" Laurie asked. "All those months — years when he wasn't there for you?"

"Oh, but he was there for me!" her mother said, quite shocked that Laurie should think otherwise. "He was always there for me — for all of us — in his heart."

Laurie was shocked and embarrassed.

To think that she hadn't been able to sense that during all those months — all those years — her father had been abroad yet still there at home, for them. All kinds of emotions raced through her mind.

For some reason, her mother sensed her confusion.

"This is really about Don, isn't it?" she said. Laurie couldn't answer at first, could only stare into her empty plate.

"I'm not like you. I couldn't handle the emptiness — his going away."

Her mother smiled tenderly, as if she longed to rush around the table and hug her, as if she so desperately wanted Laurie to know what it had taken her a lifetime to discover.

"Ah, but can you handle his never coming back . . .?" she enquired softly.

THERE were six digits — just six simple numbers. More than likely he would be away and it would be his answering machine which greeted her. She could then leave a discreet, evasive "hello" on it. A well-disguised cry for help . . .

Her trembling fingers fumbled for the numbers. There was a pause as they connected — a pause in which her nerve fled like a frightened bird. Then a brr-brr on the line sent her pulse pounding —

Put the phone down! ordered a proud but panicky voice in her head. Hold on! urged a calmer, deeper voice in her heart . . .

The brr-brr stopped — abruptly. There was a click, then that familiar voice was speaking in her ear. Suddenly her limbs seemed to be melting — like butter off a hotplate.

"Hello?"

She panicked, aching to place the receiver down, but as out of control as a

114

lemming diving over a cliff . . .

"Don . . . ?" A silly, small voice escaped her. "It's Laurie."

The silence was deafening. Her heart — a second so determined to hold on — now sank into a dull space.

"I didn't know if you'd be away — but of course you're not because you answered. I just wanted to say . . ." She was babbling and she couldn't stop. "I just want to say . . ."

What did she want to say, that she had been rash, that she had been wrong . . .?

"I just wanted to know if you're OK? I'm sure you are. I am, well fairly . . ." She waffled on, her words a tumbling stream which dried up into a humming silence.

She gripped the receiver; closed her eyes; bit her lip; and hoped . . .

It was then the thought hit her. He didn't want to talk to her!

"Laurie!" he said so urgently she jumped. Was that anger in his voice?

"Laurie!" It wasn't anger, it was relief.

"I've missed you. I've been in Lagos — for six weeks. It seemed much longer knowing you weren't there to come home to.

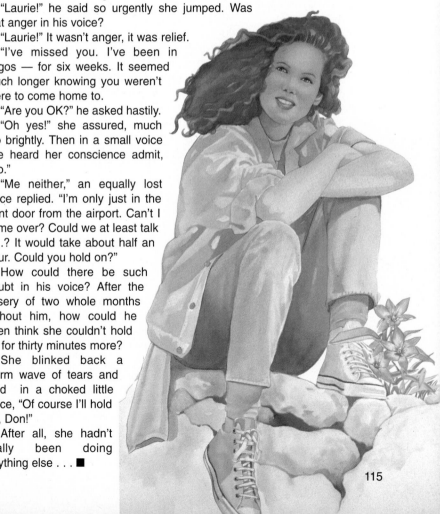

"Are you OK?" he asked hastily.

"Oh yes!" she assured, much too brightly. Then in a small voice she heard her conscience admit, "No."

"Me neither," an equally lost voice replied. "I'm only just in the front door from the airport. Can't I come over? Could we at least talk . . .? It would take about half an hour. Could you hold on?"

How could there be such doubt in his voice? After the misery of two whole months without him, how could he even think she couldn't hold on for thirty minutes more?

She blinked back a warm wave of tears and said in a choked little voice, "Of course I'll hold on, Don!"

After all, she hadn't really been doing anything else . . . ■

The Mountai

Rescue Dog

By Joyce Stranger

Inspired by an illustration by Mark Viney

Yes, we bought you, long ago. There was so much we didn't know.
Crazy pup, racing the breeze, stop and sniff beneath the trees.
Puppy with so little sense. We never thought you'd grow immense.

A year-old dog with dancing eyes, every day a new surprise.
Bark at children, chase the cat. Destroy our shoes, and tear the mat.
Hooligan, so often bad. We say, "this dog will drive us mad."

Another year, and training school. You often made me look a fool.
Until the day we took our test and your great score out-shone the rest.
Now our real work had begun. For me, a mission, for you, fun.

On the mountains, climbing steep. Concentrate, ignore the sheep.
Growing proficient, growing wise. Learning to use nose and eyes.
Often braving mountain danger, hunting for an injured stranger.

Phone rings at night, we both arise. Helicopter takes us through the skies.
In freezing dark we start our quest, doing what we both do best.
So many times we make a friend, saved from an untimely end.

Mission over, our job's done. We can relax and have some fun.
From my flask I take a drink, eat a sandwich, sit and think.
You climb above me, stand and stare, looking up into the air.

Maybe you can angels see. Visions they deny to me.
Down the mountain by my side, my special dog, my joy, my pride.
Never thought when you were young that your praises would be sung.

Your story's written on your grave. "So many lives this dog did save."
I can remember now, with pleasure, the dog that proved to be a treasure.
That picture hanging on my wall . . . My mountain dog . . . that says it all.

**Every day little Ben waited for the fox, hoping
that this time he'd make his parents
understand the magic of . . .**

His Special Visitor

By Sara Jane MacDonald

FROM where Ben lay, the sun shone through the trees above him and made leaf shadows on his bare arms and legs. He watched the patterns moving, changing, as a breeze blew the branches gently this way and that.

He could hear his mother talking inside the cottage, and away in the distance the hum of traffic. He felt peaceful lying here almost asleep in the sun. He felt the tension leave his body, and the pain in his limbs seemed to lessen.

What a view he had! Above and behind him, a beech wood rose from the garden of the cottage. Birds sang and there was a constant scurrying and movement of small creatures.

In front of him, the fields rose up behind the garden wall, fields full of sheep making their silly, fussy noises that made him want to smile.

Sometimes they would come to the patched hole in the wall and stare at him lying on his special chair-bed in the sun.

He wanted to cry out, "I'm only here because I have to be, otherwise I would be off into the woods exploring!"

But, of course, he could not cry out, and he thought that if sheep could think, they would wonder at a 10-year-old boy lying still in the sun all day.

His mother came out of the house with his sister, Sarah, carrying a drink for him.

"Hello, darling. I expect you're ready for this. I'll pull you a little more into the shade."

She helped him drink then sat beside him chatting. His sister smiled at him, and sat on the grass making daisy chains.

His mother told him of the horses she and Sarah had seen that morning — one horse so white and groomed and beautiful he must have been going to a show, and a mare so dappled and small that she seemed to merge into the deep shadows of the woods.

BEN'S eyes never left his mother's face as he listened to her quiet, cheerful voice. He loved her, loved her for knowing this place was just what he needed in the tiring weeks of physiotherapy ahead, loved her for knowing instinctively that they had to talk about horses.

He could not remember the accident, only the moments before, knowing with a sickening fear that Firelight had misjudged the gate. That was all. He could not remember his horse falling, throwing him off sideways, or beginning to roll on to him.

Ben had woken to incredible pain on a special, rippling mattress. He had been lucky, he was told — someone had managed to pull him clear, or his injuries would have been even greater.

But the worst thing of all was discovering that although he could understand what was said to him, his own words would not come out any more.

At first, only his mother had realised he could understand perfectly all that was said to him.

How she had fought for what she believed best for him!

She'd fought to have him home with her, and, with the help of a nearby hospital, organised his physiotherapy routine day after day.

Ben knew he would not have been allowed home if she had not been a physiotherapist, and she had brought him here to this lovely place to work out and to heal.

"My darling Ben," she would murmur. "It's only temporary, a little shock. In months you'll heal, body and soul together, you'll see."

He had smiled inside, the terror receding to an almost acceptable level. Even at 10, he understood the power of his mother's love.

After a while, Ben's father joined them in the garden, hugged Ben gently, then sat beside his mother on the grass. As they talked softly together, Ben fell asleep under the protective shade of the gentle, wavering beech leaves.

WHEN he awoke, it was to the mellow diffused light of early evening, and the garden was still and silent. He had been pulled from under the trees so the evening sun could warm him. He moved his body in an experimental way, stretching his legs with the steel pins in them, trying once more to move his left arm. He was almost sure feeling was coming back, that it did not hurt quite so much.

His right arm, the one that obeyed him, fell over the arm of the chair and came into contact with fur.

Surprised, because there was no cat or dog at the cottage, he turned his head and looked down.

He must be still asleep, he told himself, for lying beside him was a small fox. He closed his eyes and opened them again.

The fox was still there, watching him, panting beside him like a small brown dog, regarding him with knowing black eyes.

Ben could not believe it! He moved his fingers to touch the soft fur, and the fox stayed exactly where it was, letting itself be stroked.

Excitement flared in Ben — he found he was trying to shout out to his parents to come and look!

Sweat broke out on his forehead with the effort, but no sound came. The fox, catching his excitement, got up, shook itself, then at a movement from inside the house, turned and lolloped to the gap in the wall and began to move up the steep, curved field at an irregular run.

Ben watched until he was out of sight. Was it the same fox he saw each day, out in the field in broad daylight? How had the fox dared to come into the garden and right up to him?

WHEN his parents came out for him he moved his right hand and blinked at them with his eyes.

"What is it, Ben? What are you trying to tell us?" His father came closer, and Ben moved his head up towards the field.

Both his parents turned and looked, but there were only sheep — the small brown fox had long gone.

Tears of frustration filled Ben's eyes.

His mother looked at him intently. "Good, Ben! It's good you're trying to tell us something. Don't stop trying, darling. The words won't always be a jigsaw. They will come, believe me."

But at that moment Ben did not believe her, and he wept harsh, lonely tears into the night.

*   *   *   *

Now, each day Ben waited for the fox, and every evening she came. He knew now she was a vixen. He watched her coming closer and closer.

Then she would disappear in the dip, only to reappear through the wall and move stealthily through the lengthening shadows to his chair. She would sit watching him.

He longed to show her off, but she never came when anyone else was in the garden. He stayed awake for her and tried to form words in his head for her. The excitement of her coming to him never lessened.

Sometimes he would doze with his hand in her fur, and she seemed to doze, too, hidden from the house by his tall chair. He would try to sort the word jigsaw in his head, and the words began to form like a refrain — "Fox, Fox, Fox."

One evening, his sister approached on sandalled feet, saw them together and rushed inside calling, "Mummy, Daddy! Quick, there's a funny dog near Ben!"

His parents came flying out, but the fox had gone, quick as a shadow.

Ben was angry — now they would watch him and the fox would not come. He glared at his sister.

His mother looked thoughtful.

"Don't look cross, darling," she said. "A friendly sheepdog, was it?"

"No," Sarah said. "It wasn't a sheepdog. It was red."

"A red setter?"

"It was small and browny-red. I didn't see it properly, but it was funny."

Ben's parents exchanged glances and sent Sarah for biscuits.

"A little poetic licence, I think. Maybe she's feeling a little neglected," his mother said.

The word was forming again and again in Ben's head. It was going to burst from him like a huge bubble.

"Fox! Fox!"

It came in an unfamiliar explosion of sound, and his parents whirled round to him.

"Ben! Ben! What did you say? Come on, say it again, come on, son," his father pleaded.

"Fox." His voice was strange and croaky, as if coming from someone else. "Fox. Fox."

For a moment they both stared at him, disbelief then incredible relief on their faces. His mother burst into tears, and both his parents were hugging him, and laughing and crying at the same time.

His mother cradled his head in her arms. "You've done it! Oh, Ben!"

"Like a fox, was it, Ben? So Sarah was right," his father said.

"Fox," Ben said again, suddenly feeling very tired.

Still smiling, his father picked him up. "Foxes don't come into gardens for chats, old son, but it must look very like a fox, I grant you. Come on. Time you were in bed. You're looking very tired."

The words were not a jigsaw in his head any more. He didn't understand why but they were beginning to form correctly.

In the dark he prayed that the vixen wouldn't desert him, that she would come back. He had come to rely on her arrival.

IN the morning the words were a jumble again, and Ben was still very tired. After his morning exercises, he slept all afternoon on a rug on the grass so that he could move his arms and legs more freely. The vixen came later that evening, quietly, as shadows filled the garden, and she lay beside him on the rug panting a little.

He noticed her shape for the first time and knew she was going to have young.

Tonight she was restless, and padded about near him looking for shade. Eventually she collapsed beside him seeming exhausted.

Tentatively, Ben reached out and stroked her, and he felt her begin to relax.

Fox, he thought. My fox.

Then he dozed again.

He woke to the click of a camera, and felt the vixen shoot from under his arm and away. Looking up, he saw his parents in the doorway of the cottage.

They were excited.

"I'm sure it was a fox! It looked just like a fox," his mother said. "Didn't you see its tail?"

"Foxes are wild, love. They don't creep into gardens to visit young boys."

"It is odd, though."

"It's very odd."

They walked towards Ben.

"It is fox," he said in a croaky voice. "My fox."

"Oh, Ben!" They laughed. "Wonderful, wonderful Ben! It's so good to hear you beginning to talk again."

As they reached him, someone called from the woods and came down into their garden. She was an old lady wearing plimsolls and what looked like an evening dress.

"It's only old Jenny," she called. "Excuse me, now, but I'm looking for Heidi. She's getting near her time."

Ben's parents looked blank, but in a flash Ben realised.

"Your fox?" he said so clearly he surprised himself.

The old woman smiled at him and he felt that somehow she knew everything about him.

"Yes. They call me the Fox Woman round here. I thought Heidi might have been visiting you.

"You're doing well, much better than a few weeks ago, aren't you?" she said to Ben, already knowing the answer.

123

"So it was a fox?" his father said.

"I didn't know you could tame wild things like that," his mother added.

"Foxes are my life," Jenny explained. "Since I was a child, if I've found them abandoned or hurt in the woods, I've cared for them until they were ready to return to the wild.

"The trouble is, some don't want to leave — they become used to humans."

She waved her stick up at the woods and smiled down at Ben again. "Usually when they find a mate they forget, but not Heidi. She was so injured when I found her, that now her security is people, she loves them."

So injured. The words hung on the air in the quiet little garden.

Ben's parents turned to look at each other, and then down at their son.

"But not any more," his mother said softly.

F Jenny heard the comment she didn't acknowledge it, merely turned her attention back to Ben.

"You'll have to get on your feet and come and see Heidi's litter, won't you?" she said cheerfully.

He stared at her. "Yes . . . but . . . if . . . I can't, will . . . Heidi come again . . . to me . . . ?"

He trembled with the effort of the words.

The old woman held his gaze. "No, Ben, this time you must visit Heidi. That's only fair, isn't it?"

Ben nodded. He saw that it was only fair.

He gritted his teeth and moved his legs on the rug. It hurt, but suddenly he was sure he could do it.

He didn't see the grateful glance his parents gave the old lady, before she moved slowly away back into the woods to find her fox. ■

STRANGERS IN THE HOUSE

And to think — they were his own children!

By Sarah Burkhill

K EN couldn't remember the name of the film, but the theme kept coming back to him. It had involved the take-over of human beings by an evil power from outer space. Alien spirits had taken possession of human bodies.

Ken had watched it at Marjorie's house late on Friday night, a year or two before they were married.

125

He had enjoyed it immensely, because Marjorie had been terrified and kept moving closer and closer until, by the end, she was sitting on his knee with both arms wrapped tightly round his neck.

Now, however, 18 years later, the memory of the film gave him the creeps because it had become a reality! Two members of his household, Ken was convinced, had been taken over by aliens.

One of them was in the back bedroom this very minute, accompanied by two fellow aliens.

On his way back from the bathroom Ken paused outside the door and listened warily. Not that there was much point. They were talking in code, and he couldn't understand a word of it.

"Breaker Fourteen for a copy," a voice chanted. "Hello, hello. This is the Pickle Machine from Greenwich Village. What's your handle?"

He pressed his ear closer to the door as interference made a crackling noise, then gasped in fright as a hand gripped his shoulder.

"Ken Dixon, you should be ashamed of yourself!" Marjorie announced, frowning at him. "Eavesdropping on your own son! Really!"

Ken explained his theory about aliens, but she was not impressed.

"Stop being silly. They're playing with that CB radio Gordon gave him — as you know perfectly well!"

"Ah, but do I?" Ken retorted. "What if they're passing messages back to their controller? They could be plotting to take over the world, for all we know. They could even be —"

Marjorie raised her eyes to the heavens and went into their bedroom with a pile of neatly-folded laundry to be put away. Ken hovered outside his son's bedroom door.

It was the one calling himself Pickle Machine who was their son, Davie.

He wore an earring in his left ear, faded and baggy blue jeans and a tatty old T-shirt which should have been in the bin long ago.

He was a mess.

Because it was Saturday and there was no school, his hair was standing straight up from his head in vicious-looking spikes.

If further proof of his theory were needed, Ken thought, that was it!

He gave up trying to make sense of the CB jargon and padded downstairs to take refuge in the kitchen.

The living-room, sadly, was at present a no-go area, being inhabited by his daughter and her cronies.

Agonised wailing noises were coming from the room, but as they were accompanied by drums and guitar, Ken risked assuming it was a CD and not his daughter murdering — or being murdered by — one of the others.

There were four of them altogether. Ken had gone in an hour ago to fetch his newspaper. They had been sitting on the floor in a circle, doing each other's hair.

Another memory flashed into his head — of a trip long ago to the zoo, and four monkeys which had sat in a cage patiently grooming one another.

There, though, the similarity ended. The monkeys had at least been friendly.

The four in the front room had pointedly stopped talking and Shona had frowned irritably at him until he had collected the paper and departed.

KEN made himself a cup of coffee and settled gloomily at the kitchen table to drink it. Maybe Marjorie was right, he thought. Maybe he was just getting old, and that was why teenagers suddenly seemed like alien beings.

Last week had seen his 40th birthday.

Forty! he thought in horror. Middle age! The dreaded 4-0! Mental and physical decay just around the corner!

Maybe he really was having a mid-life crisis, as Marjorie had jokingly remarked.

All in all, though, Ken preferred the alien theory. He was in the process of expanding on it when the kitchen door opened and Marjorie came in holding a floor mop.

"What are you doing in here?" she demanded.

"Hiding," he replied.

"Well, go and hide somewhere else, dear. I want to wash the floor. Why not go into the living-room?"

"I can't," Ken complained. "They're in there!"

"Well, they won't eat you."

Ken wasn't too sure about that.

"They'll look at me, though," he protested feebly.

Marjorie gave an exasperated sigh.

"There's nothing wrong with them. They're nice kids. And Davie's pals are nice, too. The only difficult, anti-social person in the house is you!"

She brushed him aside with the mop, ruffling his hair as she passed.

"And you're just in a bad mood because it rained and you couldn't go and play golf!" she teased him.

"Humph!" Ken grunted, not bothering to contradict her.

She continued to mop round him. He edged closer to the door before he was marooned completely on a tiny island of dry floor.

"Why don't you go and watch that film you taped last week, the night we were at Gordon and Irene's?" Marjorie suggested helpfully.

"I can't," Ken said plaintively. "Shona's taped 'Neighbours' over it. Nobody cares about what I might want to see. I'm just the old guy who pays the bills. I don't matter."

"Aw, pet!" Marjorie declared in mock sympathy.

"Honestly, Ken, you're a pain in the neck when you're bored. You could go and tidy out the garage, if you can't find anything else to keep you occupied."

He wasn't that bored.

"I think," he announced loftily, "I'll go across town and see my father — see if he wants to go for a couple of pints.

"At least he listens to me," he muttered darkly as Marjorie finally succeeded in manoeuvring him out of the kitchen.

"Good idea!" she sighed in relief.

"Oh, and ask him to come over for lunch tomorrow," she called after him.

He was a great old fellow, Ken's dad. At 78 he was as fit as a flea, and spent his days running errands for "the old folk," as he called some of his less-sprightly neighbours.

Ken eased the car out of the driveway and turned down into Lincoln Avenue.

In the driving mirror, he could see Fernando the Frog sprawled on the back ledge, bulbous topaz eyes bursting from his green velvet body.

Shona had bought Fernando for him, a present from her first Guide camp at Colwyn Bay, nearly five years ago. A lucky mascot, she'd said, to protect him from danger on the roads.

Ken sighed. She had been a lovely little thing when she was younger — before she'd turned into a sullen, discontented stranger who argued with him every morning at the breakfast table over how late she'd been the night before.

ONE day, in particular, he remembered. It was during the school holidays and Shona must have been about 11. It was the first time she had been allowed to go into town on her own, and at lunchtime she had presented herself at the offices of Unwin, Lowson & Co. to take her old dad out to lunch.

She'd been wearing a pale-blue skirt and a white peasant-style blouse, with her hair tied back in bunches. He remembered it as clearly as if it were yesterday.

Old Alec Lowson had been captivated by her.

"This is your daughter?" he'd said, astounded. "And just how did an ugly brute like you manage to produce such a little treasure?"

"He's not ugly at all!" Shona had protested. "I think he's lovely!"

And she took his hand as they walked out to lunch, and Ken felt so full of pride that he could have danced all the way to the restaurant.

Now, she never seemed to have time for him at all. Now she walked about with earphones in, and all she could think about was make-up and fashion and soap operas and that stupid, discordant wailing she called music.

It was the same with Davie, too. Once upon a time, before the dreaded teens, he and Davie had done all sorts of things together.

At weekends they'd gone fishing. They'd played football in the back garden, much to Marjorie's annoyance and the detriment of her herbaceous border.

Every week night, after school, Davie had waited for him at the station, and together they'd walked the short distance back to the house, talking over their respective days.

Ken took the corner into Park Drive.

Davie didn't do that now. These days he had no time for anything except pop music, his pals, and that daft CB radio that Marjorie's brother Gordon had given him.

Not, Ken thought sadly as he parked outside his father's house, that he would even want Davie to meet him at the station — not now he looked the way he did. He didn't want anyone to see them together.

128

HUGH DIXON frowned slightly, then smiled.

"I remember that film. It was on again a couple of months ago," he announced. " 'Invasion Of The Body Snatchers!' "

"That was it!"

Ken settled back into a corner seat at the White Swan, and raised his glass in a gesture of triumph. Dad knew the film, too.

"So you see what I'm getting at?"

Dixon Senior contemplated the head on his bitter, then nodded sympathetically.

"I know, son," he murmured. "You sometimes wonder why you ever bothered in the first place. It's as if you're only there to pay the bills. As long as you installed a cash dispenser in the living-room, they wouldn't care if you

walked out tomorrow and never çame back."

"Exactly! And do you know something?" Ken went on. "That's just what I feel like doing sometimes! Walking out and never coming back, I mean."

His father's white head was nodding vigorously.

"Yes," he agreed. "You wish you could find a nice little garret somewhere, where there's no noisy music thumping away all the time, and no bodies sprawled around the place, taking up all the comfortable chairs."

"And no soap operas taped over the films you want to watch," Ken threw in, warming to his theme.

"And no sullen, impertinent faces, raising their eyes to the ceiling every time you open your mouth, as if to say, 'Oh, no, there he goes again!' "

Ken put down his glass and gazed at his father in amazement.

"That's it! That's it exactly!" he almost squeaked.

"Except when you're giving them money, of course," his father interjected.

"That's true," Ken agreed. "They occasionally manage a half smile on a Friday, as if they were doing me some kind of favour by accepting their pocket money!"

His father sniffed loudly.

"And then when they've got it they rush out and buy more abominable records to drive you mad with."

"And hair dye." Ken was working himself up to fever pitch now. "And magazines. And revolting eye make-up. And even, in Davie's case, an earring!"

He finished his drink and stared morosely into the empty glass.

"Do you want another?" his father asked gently.

"No, thanks. Better not when I'm driving."

"All right. We might as well just go back to my house, and I'll make us a cup of coffee."

In companionable silence, they walked up the road back to the semi-detached house where Ken had grown up.

"Oh, while I remember, Marjorie says you've to come to lunch tomorrow, if you're not out gallivanting."

"Very nice. I'll look forward to that, tell her."

Hugh Dixon paused at the gate.

"There's another thing," he remarked. "Isn't it annoying how women always side with the kids whatever they do?"

"How do you know that? Has Marjorie been talking to you?"

"Marjorie didn't say a word," his father insisted. "In fact, it's nearly a fortnight since I've seen her."

"Then how did you —"

"Go round the side way," Hugh Dixon interrupted as Ken made to walk up the path.

"I've been tidying out the garage. Come and see it."

"Don't tell Marjorie that, or it'll give her more ammunition against me," Ken laughed. "She's been on at me for weeks to do ours."

"Amazing what you find when you have a good old clear-out." His father opened the side door to the garage and switched on the light.

THE interior would have met with Marjorie's complete approval, Ken thought gloomily. Everything spick and span, cardboard boxes stacked neatly round the sides.

"These, for instance."

His father pulled open a box and produced a long rope of yellow wooden beads.

"Must be years since I saw those," he remarked.

"I thought you'd got rid of Mum's stuff ages ago," Ken said.

Hugh held up the beads.

"Oh, these weren't your mother's," he declared. "They were yours."

"Mine?" Ken spluttered, holding the offending necklace at arm's length.

His father continued to poke about in the box. "You had red ones, too, if I remember rightly, but I couldn't find them. They must have been thrown away."

"Yes, well, I think we —"

"But your old dress is here, though. That didn't get put out."

"Dress?" Ken squeaked.

"Yes, here it is." He pulled out a voluminous orange garment. "I remember you used to —"

"Don't be ridiculous," Ken protested. "It was a kaftan. Not a dress. I've never worn a dress in my life."

"Dress. Kaftan. Call it what you will." Hugh Dixon shrugged.

"And look!" He continued to rummage. "There's a photo of you in it."

Triumphantly he produced the faded picture. "And the yellow beads. And my marguerites from the garden in your hair."

He started to guffaw until his shoulders shook with uncontrollable mirth.

Ken ostentatiously ignored the photograph that was being thrust at him.

"Look, I don't know what you're trying to prove, but all that was entirely —"

"Flower power!" the old man said with another snort. "What year was that? Sixty-five? Sixty-six?"

"Sixty-seven," Ken said shortly. "But it's got nothing whatsoever —"

"Remember you wanted to hitchhike to San Francisco with Terry Dunlop?" He nudged Ken.

"That was where it was all happening, you said. That was where all the beautiful people went. Beautiful!" He wheezed. "You looked like something out of the 'Magic Roundabout!' What a sight!"

"Really, Dad, I wish you'd —"

"I saw you in town one day when I was out with a client, I remember," his father persisted. "I'd to drag him down a side street in case you spotted me and came over.

"I'd rather have taken a ten-mile detour than have to acknowledge you as my son and heir."

He stopped suddenly, then grinned again. "Or perhaps I should have said 'son and hair,' eh? Get it?

"Your hair was longer than Joan's when you were in your teens. I used to threaten to sneak in and cut it all off while you were asleep."

To Ken's relief he returned the kaftan, beads and photograph to the box, but

131

continued to search through the contents.

He was frowning now.

"There were some old records in here, too." He delved deeper. "Where've they gone?"

"Dad, never mind about old records —"

"It's all right. I've found them."

He examined the label of the first one. "Oh, yes, it's him. I remember him. Bushy-haired, dirty-looking creature who had trouble with his adenoids. Always seemed to sing through his nose —"

"OK, Dad," he interrupted. "I'm getting the message. Don't overdo it!"

"It's all just the same, Kenny." His father's voice was soft and his expression understanding, sympathetic even.

THEY looked at each other in silence for a moment, and a great surge of emotion welled up in Ken. If it had been his mother, he could have taken her in his arms and given her a big hug. But not his dad. You couldn't do that with your dad — not at 40.

He swallowed.

"Did I really have you feeling as bewildered, perplexed and unhappy as Davie and Shona sometimes make me?"

"More so, probably." Hugh Dixon sighed. "There were times when I'd like to have turfed you out on your ear — but of course your mother wouldn't let me.

"Women have more sense, you see. They understand these things better. She knew it was just your way of coping with growing up and that it wouldn't last for ever."

He sighed again, then went on.

"But it wasn't that I ever stopped loving you. Just — just that — well, that I was hurt. I thought I'd lost you.

"And I had, of course," he said after a moment. "We all lose our children when they get to a certain age. But we get them back again, Kenny." He brushed the dust from his hands and made to get up. "And when we do, it's usually better than ever.

"Just like . . . just like it was with you and me, son," he added, a husky edge to his voice.

Ken reached out and put an arm round the old man, to steady him as he got to his feet.

"It's all right, I can manage," Hugh Dixon said.

"I know you can." Ken squeezed his shoulder and gave him a quick, embarrassed pat on the back.

*　　*　　*　　*

"I thought you were going to make coffee?" he said gruffly.

"So I am, son. C'mon!"

Ken hummed an old Dylan song as he drove back to Churchill Drive, feeling happier than he had for a while.

Not that his problems had been resolved, really.

The weather forecast still ruled out a game of golf this weekend, and his house was still inhabited by two aliens.

The music would be just as loud and discordant when he got home as it had been when he left.

He'd still have to fight the urge to drag Shona off to the bathroom and scrub all that muck off her pretty young face.

And he'd still have pleasing fantasies about making a bonfire with Davie's entire wardrobe plus the CB radio.

But now Ken felt able to cope with all these things — because his dad had made him realise they wouldn't last for ever.

And probably in about 20 or 30 years' time, Ken would have a visit from his son and daughter.

They would sit opposite him, as he had just sat with his father, and with brows furrowed in dejection and annoyance, they would pour out a long tale of woe about their teenage offspring.

Ken smiled in gleeful anticipation.

And when that day came — boy, was he going to enjoy it! ∎

Squirrels

by Joyce Stranger

Inspired by an illustration by Mark Viney

Red coat, bright eyes and bushy tail.
A fleeting glimpse.
A pair of imps.
Not yet full grown as born this spring.
Yet they know that winters bring
Bare trees and ice and bitter cold.
They must store the autumn gold.

So they search the woodland floor,
Acorns for their winter store.
Burying them beneath the ground.
When times are hard they will be found.
Fresh and sweet these seeds will keep
Till both wake from their winter sleep.

Work now over, time for play.
Thus they break up every day.
Racing, chasing, through the trees,
Rustling bright autumn leaves.
Come the spring, they'll both be grown
And rearing families of their own.

Learning then that they must strive
Their own young to keep alive.
Their enemies they now must know.
Magpie, owl, and hawk and crow.
We long for springtime and a glimpse
Of these attractive little imps.

Wanted – One Miracle!

Deep down, Fred knew he was asking for the impossible. What he'd forgotten was that anything is possible at Christmas . . .

By Maureen Peters

EVERYBODY," Miss Burns said, "will be taking part."

Unspoken were the words, "And woe betide anyone who argues." Not that Form IIB had any intention of arguing. When Miss Burns, who was 25 going on 97, got that glint in her eyes, even the most difficult pupil co-operated, and on this occasion there was no need for the glint, anyway. Every pupil in the class wanted to be in the Nativity play.

Lots were drawn every year to see which class would have the honour of presenting the play, although the headmistress usually managed a little judicious cheating to ensure that the draw contained a sufficient amount of talent to parade before parents and visitors.

Understandably, she was unwilling to risk a repetition of one horrific year when St Joseph had punched the Archangel Gabriel for forgetting his lines and the Virgin Mary had cast aside her blue veil and joined in.

For the past five years, the performances had been decorous and charming.

136

"We will all," Miss Burns continued, "begin by reading the play aloud and then, when I have given out the parts, we will all learn our lines."

Books were opened, temporary rôles allotted, and the class settled while Miss Burns jotted down names, and considered them. Deborah McSharron would be the Virgin Mary. She had the long, fair hair and the air of sweet serenity the rôle demanded.

Tom Fenton would be Joseph. He was a solemn, responsible child who, at seven, already foreshadowed the worried-looking 40-year-old he was destined to become.

Fiona O'Grady would be ideal as the Archangel Gabriel. She was a statuesque, imposing girl for her age, anyway, and Miss Burns didn't see why a girl shouldn't play the part.

Simon Jones would be the Innkeeper. Betty Smith would be . . . Looking up, she thoughtfully surveyed her pupils. But when her eyes alighted on the small figure at the back of the room, her heart sank. She had forgotten about Fred . . .

If there was anything to be tripped over, dropped or spilled, then Fred found it. It wasn't even because he was too big for his age — he was small and thin with a head that was a bit too large in proportion to his body.

She watched Fred now, staring at her blankly, his copy of the play upside down on his desk, his mop of ginger hair hanging down into his eyes. She was sure he could do better if she could only find something to capture his interest. But she seemed to have tried everything already . . .

BUT he would have to be fitted in somewhere. Desperately Miss Burns ran her eye down the cast of characters again. Third shepherd? No. Third shepherd had a line to say and Fred would never remember it. Angelic chorus?

Fred couldn't sing, though his voice drowned everybody else's when it was raised in the singing lessons.

Still, she had to find something . . . Meantime she clapped her hands for silence.

"I will now give out the parts,' she announced brightly. "Make a note of who you are supposed to be and then you'll be able to see how much you have to learn.

"Remember every part is very important. Debbie, you'll play the Virgin Mary, and Tom will play Joseph . . ." She went on down the cast list to the Magi, Bertha the servant, and the customers at the inn.

Fred's eyes were still fixed on her with an expression of innocent hopefulness.

"Fred." Miss Burns paused and then went on desperately. "There is to be a — a special part that you will play, but the details aren't worked out yet."

Fred knew that there wasn't really any part for him at all. He couldn't read words very well, but he could read people's expressions. He'd learned that quite quickly.

He knew how clumsy and awkward he could be. "Accident prone" his mum always said. He wasn't sure exactly what that was — except it meant him.

Mum would be disappointed he hadn't been given a part. He and Mum had been by themselves ever since Dad had left. It was cosy, but it also meant that Mum only had him to fuss over.

When he got home from school, she always wanted to know every detail of his day, and on the rare occasions he obtained a merit mark or a tick she acted as if he'd won a medal.

She'd been so excited at the news that his class was going to put on the play this year.

"It'll be a bit of an evening out for me," she'd said happily. "And I'll be so proud to see you on the stage."

And now it didn't look as if he was even going to be involved in it, never mind on the stage.

The bell rang and the orderly class was instantly transformed into a stampeding horde.

In the playground the air was as sharp as needles and there was a faint sparkle of frost on the asphalt. The rest of the class became part of everybody else, jumping, skipping, talking in groups.

Fred hung back, hugging the shadow of the school wall, trying not to be noticed. He didn't want any of the rest commenting on the fact that he was the only one who hadn't been given a part yet. He stood against the wall, his hands deep in his pockets, a nonchalant expression on his face.

Through the open window of the staff-room above him, Miss Burns's voice drifted.

"It was stupid of me not to have thought it out more carefully before I gave out the parts. I want to fit him in somewhere, but my mind went absolutely blank. Any suggestions?"

"Make him an understudy?" That was Miss Walton, who taught Form IIIA. Fred wondered what an understudy was. Not that it mattered because Miss Burns replied immediately. "No, that wouldn't work. He'd guess it was just to make him feel involved . . . Anyway, it isn't the same as actually being on the stage.

"But there must be something . . ." Miss Burns sounded worried. Fred was sorry about that because he liked Miss Burns.

"What you need," Miss Walton replied wryly, "is a miracle."

T HEY had been talking about miracles the week before in class. People who couldn't walk suddenly started running round, blind people could see, and ugly ducklings turned into swans. "A miracle is a gift," Miss Burns had said.

So how did he go about getting a miracle? Fred moved thoughtfully away, wishing he'd listened to the rest of the lesson. Anyway, asking for miracles didn't get very good results or Mum would win the big prize at the bingo.

"If you don't give you don't get." The words, an echo of his mother's philosophy, popped unbidden into his head.

"No good asking for an ice-cream if you haven't helped me lay the table," she'd say. "You'll never get to be Monitor if you don't help Miss to give out the pencils."

The problem was that he hadn't anything to give in exchange for even a tiny miracle.

He'd spent his pocket money on comics, lost his king marble to Dennis and the stick of chewing gum in his pocket didn't seem much to offer to whoever granted miracles in return.

By this time Fred had plodded halfway round the school grounds and was standing at the open door of the gymnasium. Usually it was locked at break, but Mr Evans the caretaker must have forgotten.

Fred wandered in and looked without enthusiasm at the vaulting horse and parallel bars.

At the back of the gym were the bits and pieces of scenery that had been brought out of storage again for the nativity play.

There was also a stool, a box of props full of things like a plastic loaf of bread and a bunch of oranges, and an inn door made of hardboard, a large, glittering star fixed to a pole, and an empty, wooden manger. There'd be a big doll put in there on the night, wrapped up in a shawl.

Of course there had been a real baby in the beginning, and Mary had wrapped Him up and put Him in the manger and sung songs to Him.

Fred wondered what had happened after they got home and Mary went out to do the shopping.

Probably Joseph had had to look after the Baby. Play with Him and sing to Him, or maybe even whistle to make the Baby laugh. He'd seen a TV programme once about a man who could whistle like all the different birds.

Later, he'd practised in his bedroom, but he hadn't been as good as the man on the TV. Even so, now he pursed his lips, and blew the sweet trilling of a nightingale towards the empty manger.

In the playground, Miss Burns, hurrying back to class after dealing with two feuding infants, stopped dead, her ears filled with a melody more beautiful than she had ever heard in her life. It was coming from the gym — she crossed to the open door and peeped in.

She'd never experienced a miracle before and the shock of it sent a chill as cold as winter rippling down her spine . . .

*　*　*　*

It was generally agreed that the play was a great success. None of the angels fought and the beards of the Magi didn't fall off. But the high spot of the performance was the very last scene when the lights dimmed over the Holy Family and Gabriel held the star as high as he could reach.

Then, in a shadowy corner an angel with untidy red hair filled the stable with nightingale song until, for one brief moment, even Miss Burns felt the gentle finger of eternity beckon. ■

140

"Remember Me...?"

The child who'd been abandoned was now a man searching for the one person who could tell him why.

By T. Ashby

THERE was plenty of time for thought on the long bus journey into Middlebridge. Time for reflection and to allow myself to wonder if what I was doing was right. It was not the action of a rational adult which, after all, was exactly what I was supposed to be.

For this whole day I had stolen for myself alone, and it was one based entirely on deceit.

Even my wife, Miriam, believed me to be at work, and I had gone through the charade of letting her drive me to the office, then waving until she was out of sight before making my way to the bus station.

I stared out of the window. The road we were

travelling along was high and narrow, and I looked down on bright yellow fields and a sparkling blue river. Dotted about the landscape were various farm buildings, a tractor being followed by a swarm of hungry, screeching gulls and in the distance, the lonely figure of a man walking a black dog.

Above me the sky was blue, flawed only by the vapour trail of a high-flying jet.

I suppose, in order to make any sense of today, I had to go back a good 17 years to when I was five years old.

*   *   *   *

I remember sitting on the edge of a hard bed as my mother buckled my brown shoes and tugged my loose grey socks up to my knees.

I was a scrawny little boy and, up until then, I had spent most of my life closeted in the dismal room while my mother went out in search of casual work.

There was one sash window in our room, but it would not open, and on hot summer days the room would be like an oven.

I COULD read quite well by the age of five, and that was how I filled my empty hours, with books my mother had borrowed from the library and listening to the little radio she had bought cheaply at the market. I wore shorts which had been cut down from trousers I had worn through at the knees and a black blazer my mother had bought at a rummage sale.

I clutched the floppy grey rabbit my mother had knitted for me, stuffed with old stockings and losing its shape.

It had red button eyes and a crooked mouth, but I loved him better than anything else and even today, he has pride of place in my bedroom beside my wife's best-loved teddy.

My cheeks burned like red-hot coals and unwanted tears pricked at my eyes. I longed for my mother to hug me, say everything was all right and stop this strained silence which had dominated since she'd woken me at dawn.

SHE didn't, of course, and grasping my hand in hers, tugged me down the uncarpeted stairs and into the bustling street outside. "Make sure you behave yourself," she said brusquely. "And don't forget to brush your teeth every day."

I was bundled into a London taxi and sat beside her, watching as her thin fingers toyed with the handles of the canvas bag which contained all my belongings.

I felt very confused. Surely she would be there to remind me. Surely going to school — for that is where I was convinced I was going so early in the morning — meant that I would come home at night. It said so in the books I read, but I was too afraid to ask, too afraid, even then, of the truth.

The thought of travelling normally thrilled me, and this was my first ever ride in a taxi, or in any car come to that. But that day I neither saw nor felt anything.

At last the car pulled to a halt outside a tall grey building and my mother handed my bag to a woman I'd never seen before. Then she crouched down and put her hands on my shoulders.

"I . . . I can't explain," she told me, "and you probably wouldn't remember what I have to say, anyway. But . . . I do love you, Tommy. I hope you'll always remember that and remember, too, that I'm doing the right thing . . . for both of us."

What did she mean? I didn't like the way the strange woman was gripping my hand, and when my mother turned and ran — yes, she actually ran away down the street — I tried, oh how I tried, to chase after her.

Even at a distance, I could hear her crying and I think it was then it hit me that she wasn't coming back, not at teatime, not ever.

I fought, kicked and struggled, and the dreadful blazer was ripped, but I didn't care. The woman paid the taxi driver and took me inside the grey building.

"You're to wait here, Thomas," she told me kindly. "Someone will be coming for you."

MY soon-to-be adoptive parents arrived shortly after and spoke in hushed whispers to the woman who'd taken me away from my mother. They took me home with them and, strangely, I can't recall my first days with them. I think I was so torn up inside with grief, wanting no-one but my mother, that I neither saw nor felt anything for a long time, apart from the forlorn hope every time the doorbell rang that it was her, at last, come to take me home . . .

DOUG and Rose were young, and from the start I never looked on them as parents, but kindly friends whom I grew, over the years, to love. It's strange, but I can't remember when I stopped jumping up every time someone came to the door. It wasn't until I was 13 years old that I began to wonder about her again.

Why had she left me?

Why didn't she come back for me, and why couldn't I remember an older man in my life? Other people had fathers, I had Doug, but it wasn't the same.

Telling me the truth must have been a very difficult decision for my adoptive parents to make, and when Doug sat down beside me to explain, I was numbed.

"Your mother was my sister, a year younger than me," he said. "You were born when she was sixteen. She'd run away from home and no-one knew where she'd gone or even that you existed until she called me one night a few years later.

"She was desperate . . . she hadn't been able to pay the rent on your room for weeks and the landlord was threatening to turf you out on the streets. She wanted me to take care of you and, of course, I said I would.

"So, she arranged to leave you somewhere safe in London and promised to ring me and let me know where you were. I tried to persuade her to come home, to her family, but she was in such a state . . .

"I just hoped that one day she'd realise that we love her and come home."

"But she didn't," I said, fighting back the tears in my eyes.

"No, son," Doug said sadly. "She never did."

It made him my uncle, and the people I called Nan and Grandpa my real grandparents . . . "Do you know where she is now?" I asked hopefully.

"She calls occasionally to ask after you," he told me, evading my question.

I knew Doug too well, even then. He knew where she was. He was hiding it from me, but he wasn't the sort of man who would tell a lie.

I FELT so guilty, searching through his bureau with a torch in the dead of night like a common thief, but I found what I was looking for. A letter from my mother saying that she had married a good man who knew nothing of her past . . . and must never find out.

She wanted to put all that behind her, she said. She mentioned, too, a stay in hospital after a breakdown.

I scribbled the address on to a piece of paper and hid it, but I could never bring myself to make the journey to Middlebridge.

Sometimes I would feel so aggrieved at her disclaiming me, that I wanted to go there, just to punish her and destroy the happiness she had obviously found without me. Then I would want to be rid of her memory and forget she ever existed as she had apparently forgotten me.

* * * *

I blinked as the bus suddenly went through a narrow lane and the branches of trees hit the windows, making me jolt back into the here and now.

I was nearly there and I still didn't know what I would say to her when we finally met.

"Hello, Mum, remember me? I'm Tom, your son."

Or: "Do you know who I am?"

Or just: "Hello, Mum."

I even envisaged her own reaction. I imagined that she would be delighted and at the same time, I worried that she would burst into tears and accuse me of ruining her life.

I wondered if, at the back of my mind, I still wanted to hurt her for not loving me.

THE bus pulled up in a village and the driver looked over his shoulder at me.

"Middlebridge," he called. Quickly, I got off and stood for a moment, absorbing all around me.

It was a lovely little place with a wide main street and low buildings. I walked a little way and turned into a shady lane where the sun dappled the dry ground.

I don't know quite what I was expecting to find down that lane, but after our dismal, dark existence in London, it certainly wasn't the ring of childish happy laughter.

I stopped beside a low hedge and saw a small, but pretty cottage, all but hidden behind honeysuckle and yellow roses.

The large garden seemed mostly given over to lawn, scattered with brightly-coloured children's toys. There was a swing, a slide, all the things I had longed for until I'd gone to live with Doug and Rose.

In the centre of the lawn was an upturned sunbed, draped with an old blanket to form a makeshift tent. As if they sensed my presence, two little faces peeped out and I couldn't help smiling.

A man appeared from behind the cottage, puffing lazily on a pipe, his shirt sleeves rolled up to his elbows.

"Hello there," he called out as he came closer. He had a beard and laughing grey eyes. Had I remained with my mother, this man would have become my stepfather.

But deep down, I knew that had my mother kept me with her, she would never have met him.

"Lovely garden," I said, wanting to strike up a conversation.

The two children ran over to the hedge, grinning impishly up at me. They were aged about two and four, and the little girl wore blue denim dungarees, her head a cloud of unruly golden curls. The little boy was plump and stocky, his hair bleached white by a summer spent playing in the sunshine.

Strange, but I had never thought of her having more children — a half brother and sister for me.

It was an idyllic scene, one I had longed to be part of for so long, one I now knew I could never complete. For I was an outsider and my presence would only destroy the order of things.

Suddenly, I knew I had to get away. I couldn't face seeing her, I couldn't bear to spoil the happiness she'd found.

"You're not from these parts," the man said suddenly, trapping me.

"No." I shook my head. "I'm from Dewchester."

"Oh yes." The man nodded. "On holiday here, are you?"

"Just visiting," I said truthfully.

It had come to me in a flash.

All the things that these children had were the things I had had with Doug and Rose. They had given me a splendid childhood and it was only myself who marred it by retaining unhappy memories.

I had had a swing and often used to drape a blanket over the clothes line to make a tent which I would share with Doug's daughter, Alison, who was three years younger than me.

When I had once asked why they only had the one child, Rose had laughed and hugged me.

"Bless you, Tom," she said, "we only ever planned two children and that's just what we have."

I had been a fool, a blind, stupid fool. I turned to go, but stopped in my tracks as my mother came out of the cottage.

SHE looked at me, then turned uneasily to her husband.

"This young man is visiting the area," he said, then pointing the end of the pipe at the garden, added, "He was admiring the garden."

My mouth was dry. I had longed for this moment, to be face-to-face with her, and now it was happening, I just couldn't think of a single thing to say. All those clever speeches I had rehearsed . . . where were they now? I could think of nothing.

The biggest favour I could do her would be to turn around and go.

"Hello." She smiled.

My heart seemed to cease beating. That smile. My mother's dear, sweet, familiar smile, I remembered it so well . . .

All the bad memories suddenly faded and I recalled instead her tireless efforts to teach me to read and write . . . Our outings to the recreation ground where she would push me on the swings.

I remembered, too, her weariness at the end of the day; working so hard, just to give us a home.

She had left me at the home for Doug and Rose, not because she didn't want me, not because I was a hindrance to her, but because she loved me. She did the best . . . the only thing she could for me, and I owed her only my gratitude, and the right to keep her secret.

"I must go now . . . catch my bus . . ." I stammered and turning, hurried back down the lane the way I had come.

Her soft brown eyes had been like a reflection of my own. They bore that same look. She was as haunted as I was by a past neither of us could ever forget.

Silly tears stabbed my eyes. Tears, me — a grown man?

My throat felt dry and swollen, and when I tried to swallow I made a ridiculous, gulping sound.

The reason I'd made this journey would never be explained, the fact that my mother was about to be a grandmother.

I turned out of the lane into the brilliant sunshine of the main village street. I had an hour to wait for my bus, the longest hour of my life . . .

I sat down on the bench and stared across the street.

Suddenly, I heard footsteps tapping along the path towards me. I hardly dared to look, but I recognised those busy little steps of hers. She was always in a hurry, always had so much to do.

I looked up.

"Tommy," she called, tears running down her face. "Tommy, have you time to stay for a cup of tea?"

I jumped to my feet and hurried back to meet her.

All the time in the world, Mum, my heart cried, all the time in the world. ■

REMEMBEI

LOVE...

Daily, he retreated further into his own world. What would happen to their marriage if she could no longer reach him?

By Dorothy L. Garrard

THE Valentine card was waiting for Marian when she entered the classroom. Primary three seemed oblivious to the three-foot-high card propped against her desk.

Nineteen heads were bent studiously, in a kind of quietness generally alien to seven and eight-year-olds, and to any area which contained Barney Field, in particular.

As she closed the classroom door behind her, Marian sensed the atmosphere thick with excitement and suppressed giggles, and made a valiant effort to set aside the memory of the bad start to the day with Charles.

The Valentine, standing half open on the floor, was constructed, at a guess, from two sides of a cardboard packing case, and white wrapping paper with red hearts was glued all over it.

149

A piece of red ribbon was looped round the spine and tied in a crooked bow, and from the limp look of it, the whole class had had a go tying it properly.

All the eyes were on her now, squinting from beneath fringes and over the edges of books as she walked over to the card and inspected it.

It was not, in fact, a total surprise. Pursuing a rolling Biro, alone in the classroom a few days previously, she had discovered the object, as yet incomplete, tucked out of sight behind a cupboard.

She walked all around the Valentine, then pushed it open with both hands.

The inside was lined with cartridge paper from the craft cupboard and one page was covered with names and drawings.

The verse on the other page, inscribed in multi-coloured crayon and a wide variety of scripts (she guessed they'd done a few letters each), read:

Roses are red
Violets are blue
Dear Mrs Harper
We love you.

"Well, well," she said solemnly at last. "What have we here? Is it a bird? Is it a plane? Why no — it's a Valentine!"

The class exploded out of their seats, shrieking with laughter. They crowded round, tugging at her arms and her skirt, to attract her attention to their own particular contribution.

"Miss — Miss — I drawed that heart with stripes."

"I drawed my cat and he's called Valentine."

"And I drew a rose, 'cause you like roses, don't you, Miss?"

BARNEY FIELD elbowed his way to the fore, carelessly treading on feet and eliciting indignant protests.

"It was my idea! I got the box to make it from the warehouse up our road, as well!"

Marian hoped he'd asked for it. His escapades had led him into deep water more than once.

He was allowed to stay up till all hours and watch anything and everything on TV, not because he was spoiled but because nobody seemed to care.

He was more away from school than in attendance and she'd been wondering why he hadn't missed a day lately. Now she knew.

He'd doubtless been organising everybody.

"No, it wasn't your idea, it was Mr Sansome's," Susie Wallis retorted. Susie, with two brothers either side of her in age, was the only person qualified to take on Barney.

"It was mine as well, and I got the box!" Barney shouted.

"Well, I got the hearts paper from our shop and Samson got the other paper and the ribbon and . . ."

"Mr Sansome!" Marian reminded them, but Susie was in full cry.

"And all you did, Barney Field, was to order us about and upset the glue and laugh at all the things we'd written and say they were soppy!"

"Be that as it may." Marian put a gentle but restraining hand on the shoulders of the two protagonists, glaring at each other, arms akimbo. "You all made a wonderful job of my card. It's the loveliest, biggest and best Valentine I've ever had in my life.

"I'll take it home tonight and stand it in my living-room, then I can look at it all evening. Thank you very much, all of you.

"Now, back to your desks or we'll never get any work done today." They trailed reluctantly back to their places.

Now the fun was over, she felt absurdly near to tears. Her nerves, usually so steady she scarcely knew she had any, were on edge.

Charles never remembered Valentine's Day at the best of times, but he had woken to a bad day, the third in a row. He only used his wheelchair when all else failed, and this morning she'd left him in it under violent protest.

He'd resisted until she'd lost her temper — also alien to her — feeling she couldn't leave him without some means of mobility.

Hopefully, the worst of the attack would be over by tonight and the Valentine would prove a diversion.

She could point out the names and tell him a story about each interesting little individual, and maybe tomorrow things would be on an even keel again.

Until . . . the traitorous thought crept in . . . next time. Traitorous because she had married him knowing full well what the future held, and scoffed at any idea that she may not be up to the challenge.

The class had settled down by now, tongues poking from the corners of their mouths as they clutched their pens and breathed heavily over exercise books.

Marian glanced at the Valentine again, trying to hold on to the moment of pleasure, then suddenly her heart looped the loop.

FROM among the multitude of inscriptions and pictures, a drawing which she hadn't noticed before, leaped out at her. A man in a caveman-style costume with bulging muscles, lifting a heart above his head. He had long hair down to his waist. Samson.

None of the children were dextrous enough to have drawn that, and Mike Sansome knew he'd been Samson to the children ever since he arrived as supply teacher six months ago.

Mike's own hair was short, dark and curling, his athletic good looks at variance with his lazy-eyed smile.

Annoyed with herself, Marian tried to still the swift beating of her heart.

To the children the drawing was just a funny picture. But Marian knew with a sure feminine instinct that although Mike had never said a word out of place, he was more than interested in her.

It was there in the way his eyes lingered, trying to look right into her mind.

I like you a lot, Marian, they said . . . Could there be more?

As a well-balanced woman in her 30s, she could have handled that situation — as she had several times in the past.

Her delicate, pointed features, brought to life by alert, grey-green eyes and hair so fair and lightly curled, had always attracted admirers.

But it had been Charles all along from the moment they'd met, and it was still only Charles, even when they'd been shattered by the prognosis for what had started with stiffness and some unexpected stumbling.

YOU'RE looking at a cripple," Charles had said brutally. "You'd better find someone else to marry."

"You still look the same to me as you did yesterday. How dare you try to kick me out of your life!" She'd matched his tone, arms crossed in the room where the specialist had left them together.

For a second, his eyes had flickered, then became bright steel again. "I'm not kicking. Just showing you the way out."

"It's only two months since you proposed to me."

"I take it back."

"You'll have to fight me for the ring. It's staying right where it is, on my engagement finger."

He'd been lying back on the pillows, drained after painful tests, but glaring at her stubbornly. She'd stood over him, glowering back.

Inside, he'd been shouting, "I need you!" She was sure of it, yet even more sure he would never acknowledge it.

She knew him so well.

Charles had shrugged. "Please yourself. Keep it as a memento of what might have . . ."

She'd laughed abruptly over the shake of his voice. "Thanks very much, but I don't keep gifts under false pretences. I've already decided on the wedding date, so it's tough luck, Charles."

Later, a taxi had taken them back to Charles's flat.

"Thanks for the support, Marian. You've been . . . a true friend. Will you go now, please?"

"Only if you promise not to change the locks or shut me out in any way. Otherwise, I'll camp right here on your sofa and scandalise the neighbours."

"Marian." He'd turned his head away wearily. "You're twenty-four. I'm twenty-eight. Think!

"This isn't a death sentence, it's life imprisonment. How do you feel about forty years or more?"

"You talk as if there's nothing to make life easier. There's plenty, and we'll find it. Being without you would be a life sentence for me, anyway."

"How on earth would I keep a wife?" he'd asked roughly. "I'm certainly not going to live on your wages."

"The same way you'll keep yourself. If I know you, you certainly won't give up your work at the College of Music unless you have to.

"Then there'll be private tuition, as and when you feel like it. All right — there could be lean times — but I'd have kept on my teaching job, anyway."

"You realise they may be the only children you'll ever have?" He'd seemed determined to be as brutal as possible.

"I didn't say I'd marry you for your children, Charles. I love you."

"Look, just go away and think about it," he'd said.

"Only if you promise . . ."

"All right! All right!"

And she'd won, through sheer obstinacy, founded on the certainty of his love for her.

The commitment for better or worse had been there right at the start of their brief courtship, from the moment Charles had crossed the room to her at a social function and said gruffly — "I can't dance, but will you sit this one out with me . . .?"

HIS proposal had been equally prosaic. "That would be a nice place for us to buy a house," he'd said, pointing to a riverside development from the hill where they were resting during a hike. "I wouldn't disturb the neighbours with my piano."

From his trouser pocket, from among the loose change, he had produced an antique ring with a square-cut emerald which had belonged to his mother.

"See if it fits. It's got character, not like this modern junk."

It fitted. She continued the hike, wearing it, half unsure as to whether she was engaged or not.

If he remembered her birthday, he gave her books and records still in their paper bags.

Yes, there had been times of laughter, and even forgetfulness of what lay ahead.

But as they years went by, he had built such a barrier against emotional weakness, that Marian felt she was on the wrong side without a gap to squeeze through.

MARIAN tore her eyes from that tell-tale caricature at the bottom of the Valentine. She had not dealt as properly with the Mike Sansome situation as she had with the others. In fact, she hadn't dealt with it at all, allowing it to remain like a secret escape route which she had no intention of using.

Mike had come along at a particularly opportune time, when the doubts she had utterly refuted for 12 years began to erode her shining confidence. She was grateful for his pleasant, amusing conversation.

When his dark eyes appreciated a new dress which Charles hadn't even noticed, she felt a guilty release of tension and a glimpse of the lighter side of life.

So, although she sensed possible danger ahead, she allowed herself to be warmed and comforted.

The thought of another difficult evening trying to breach the barrier to the desperate, angry Charles inside the strait-jacket of his infirmity, weighed lighter for the presence of that absurd Samson, with his knees bowing under the weight of the proffered heart.

"Who's a popular girl, then?"

Mike's voice startled her so much that she dropped her desk lid with a clatter, the noise echoing through the empty classroom.

"I'm told it was your idea."

He grinned. "I heard Susie chattering on about the Valentine cards in her mother's shop. It really stemmed from that. Appropriate for craft lessons, I thought, and it certainly kept them quiet — except for Barney Field, of course, but his box did come in handy."

"Thanks for the thought, anyway, Mike. It certainly brightened my day."

"Surely it wasn't the only one you had?" He was too quick by half to read her tone.

She laughed brightly. "Charles isn't into these things. Cards are only the trimmings on a good thing, anyway, aren't they?" she excused him.

"Oh, come on, Marian, you're much too young to dismiss life's frivolities like that! I had a feeling you needed cheering up. Purple shadows don't go with your beautiful eyes."

His tone was light but his steady gaze made her look away.

"A good night's sleep will work wonders," she replied, ignoring the intent look. "Meanwhile, do you think you could possibly give me a lift home with this work of art? My car's in for an MOT."

At her door, he said, "One good turn deserves another, wouldn't you say?

154

My stint at Dawley Street finishes next week. Will you have dinner with me tomorrow night?"

Getting out of the car, Marian glanced involuntarily towards the bungalow. It was on the riverside estate, but not the house Charles had planned. This one had ramps.

"I wouldn't call having dinner with you a good turn, exactly," she demurred.

"Oh, but it is. I hate eating out alone."

"You don't have to eat out!" she countered.

"Oh, but I do sometimes. Another of life's delightful frivolities, you know?"

How long had it been since she'd eaten out, seen wine winking in the candle light?

"You must have plenty of women friends who aren't married," she reminded.

"Being married doesn't prevent you having a farewell meal with a friend, surely, in this age of liberated woman?"

"No, but —"

"Good." Mike grinned. "I'll book a table at a nice country inn. We'll go straight from school, have a drive and make it a long, relaxed evening. It'll do you the world of good!"

"Mike —"

But he'd slammed the car door and roared away, leaving her on the path with her Valentine.

She stood it on the doorstep and fumbled for her key. She could hear Charles at the piano, and recognised the music with some astonishment.

He usually preferred the majestic or the military, with the same implacable strength of his own nature.

Now, a Chopin sonata was delicately threading its way like spun silver throughout the house, but as her key turned in the lock, he crashed into Wagner without a pause, drowning her in thunder.

"Look what the class made me." She laughed, but the notes rang into silence. She knew better than to question him about his day when he wore that tight-wired look round his eyes.

AFTER dinner she told him anecdotes about the kids, exaggerated for fun or effect. But not even Barney's tale, about the stray mongrel which had attached itself to him at the dump, and which he fed on chips and the smuggled remains of his dinner, brought about any relaxation in Charles's expression.

Weary and dispirited, she got up to make the evening drinks earlier than usual. For all the communication going on, she might as well have been alone in the house.

"I'll make my drink later. I've been asleep most of the day," Charles said briefly. "You can go to bed if you want to. I can manage now."

She went without arguing.

Lying in bed, staring into the darkness, her absolute faith in his love for her faltered for the first time.

On what foundation had she built it? When, in fact, had he ever said he loved her?

She had bulldozed him into marrying her, into keeping his promise — or rather, his intimidated intention. All along, he'd done his utmost to manage without her, as if that was what he really wanted.

Mike's face kept slipping into her mind's eye. She thought longingly of candlelight blurring the hard edges of reality, of a meal she didn't have to prepare, and light, frivolous conversation which wasn't fraught with pitfalls.

There really couldn't be any harm . . . if Charles comes to bed before I sleep, I won't go, she promised herself, but before she had another thought, it was morning.

When Mike told her he'd booked a table at the Millwheel, some 15 miles out into the country, she compromised by saying he could pick her up after she'd prepared Charles's own meal.

She told Charles she was having dinner with a colleague who was leaving. He didn't ask questions, he probably assumed it was a kind of party, like others before it.

"If you don't want me to go, I won't," she said, hesitating by the door, in the dress she'd bought with Charles in mind. The only compliment he'd ever paid her was to tell her that the particular shade of jade green was her colour.

"Don't be silly."

"I won't be late."

"Go and enjoy yourself."

SHE didn't know what to make of that. His voice was a matter of fact, yet something in it disturbed her. But Mike tooted his horn outside, and with a last smile, she left him.

In the low-slung sports car she felt like a girl again. The emotions she had scarcely experienced before Charles came along surged through her in a tumbling tide.

They were different emotions to what she felt for Charles — excitement, anticipation, and an almost adolescent thrill when Mike smiled at her.

The evening lay ahead like a deep, dangerous stretch of water, into which she could tumble and drown. Or, unless she was very careful, could even dive into of her own accord . . .

There was a slight hold-up beyond the traffic lights, and a knot of people by the roadside just round the corner. They seemed perturbed.

"Do you think there's been an accident?" Marian asked anxiously.

"It's just a dog," Mike said with a quick glance, picking up speed.

Marian grasped his arm.

"Mike — stop! There's Barney!"

Marian ran back to where Barney was heaving his pet on to the pavement. Nobody was helping, because Barney — looking his usual nobody-cares-and-nor-do-I unkempt self — was yelling at them all to keep away, in language which made her wince.

He heard it every day at home, of course.

156

"Barney!" She touched his shoulder.

"Get off!" Barney roared, struggling free. "Nobody's touching my dog! Leave us be!"

"Barney — it's me — Mrs Harper. Let me help."

He looked up at her blindly. There were no tears, but the helpless fear in his eyes made her own hot and prickly.

"Tiger's all right! He's going to be all right!"

Anything less like a tiger, Marian had yet to see. The animal was small and thin, with a rough coat which matched Barney's hair.

Its eyes were closed and blood matted the hair along its gashed side. One foreleg was plainly broken.

"I'll get Mr Sansome."

She ran back to Mike. "The dog's badly hurt, we must get him to the vet. There's a clinic in Vicarage Road."

She put Barney and the dog into the back seat, over which Mike had thrown a newspaper. The child's fingers were twined in the dog's fur, as if he was determined not to be parted from it.

"Where are we going, Miss?"

"To the PDSA, to see a vet."

IKE drove fast, cornering so sharply that Marian frowned. Highly attuned to moods, she sensed there wasn't much patience in Mike's. He helped lift the dog up the steps with his hands under its haunches, at a distance.

"Don't look at me like that, Marian," he said tersely. "I just don't see the point in ruining my suit as well as your dress."

She put a calming arm round Barney's shaking shoulders when the dog was taken into the surgery, even though she expected him to fling it aside. Instead, he sat rigid, staring across the room at nothing. Wiping his hands on his handkerchief, Mike went over to the window.

After some time, the vet emerged. He smiled at Barney. "Your dog — what's his name —?"

"Tiger."

"Tiger's going to be all right. But he'll need a lot of care."

His wise eyes assessed the little boy, then went to Marian.

"The dog's been neglected, I know. He was a stray, you see," Marian explained. "But I'll see to him. And to the bill, of course," she added, giving her name and address.

"Is that all right, Barney — if I have Tiger at my house until . . . well, he really can't go back to the dump, you know?"

Barney said in a trembling, most un-Barney-like voice, "My dad said he won't have him."

"I'll talk to him. If he still doesn't want to, then we'll think of something else. Don't worry, Barney, you won't lose Tiger."

"Marian — do you really want to lumber yourself with it . . .?" Mike warned, then suddenly Barney began flailing his arms. His balled fists missed Marian

157

by a hair's breadth and she started back, alarmed. Until she recognised his expression.

Mike sprang forward as though to grab Barney.

"No, Mike!"

Her eyes locked with Barney's in sudden, shocking comprehension.

Tears, probably the first Barney had ever shed since infancy, began flowing down his dirty face in rivers.

"Miss — Miss!" he choked, and buried his head in the crook of her arm. Telling her everything for which he had no words, only familiar gestures of defence. Thank you. Thank you. I love you.

Holding him, Marian felt all the muddled jigsaw pieces of emotion drop into place, jarred into a pattern which made beautiful sense.

Circumstances — life — had conspired against Barney as they had against Charles. But behind the barriers they'd built for self preservation, all the feelings were there, building up, ready to be released like a shriek through a safety valve.

She shivered, stroking the child's tousled head, letting him cry himself out in the haven of her compassion.

When he stopped, he ceased abruptly and, with a great hiccup, wiped his face dry on his sleeves.

"We'll run you home, Barney," Mike said immediately. "And I'll phone the Millwheel to hold the table. You'll want to change, Marian."

"Mike —"

She watched Barney marching down the steps, his own man again and fiercely independent.

"It's all off, isn't it?" Mike said flatly.

"I'm sorry. But it'll take time to explain to Mr Field — I can't just leave . . ."

"You don't have to give me excuses, Marian. I'd have lost anyway."

"Lost?" she asked, though she knew what he meant. "Was there a contest?"

"No," Mike replied dryly. "No contest at all."

CHARLES got to his feet when she walked in, grasping the piano to steady himself. He looked horrified.

She had forgotten the crumpled state of her frock, the blood and the dirt. She crossed quickly to him, kneeling beside him as he sat again, laying her face in his lap.

She hadn't done that for a long time.

"Are you OK?" he asked.

"I'm fine. Barney's mongrel nearly met his end, though. I didn't go to dinner after all. I've been trying to sort things out for Barney."

She told him about it. Across the room, from the corner of her eye, she could see the drawing of Samson, posturing with his heart.

She looked up into Charles's face.

"Mr Field isn't a dog lover. How'd you feel about a canine lodger with a regular visitor to take him for walkies? We did talk about having a dog once, remember?"

Charles's hands still gripped the chair arms.

"What would those kids do without you?"

"Get used to someone else, no doubt. They're resilient. What would you do without me, Charles?"

She felt him tense with apprehension. She knew his head turned to look at the card. Of course he hadn't missed a thing. Charles knew her so well.

His unspoken question hung in the air.

Are you leaving me, Marian. Are you?

She waited, praying. As with Barney, only a crisis would smash that barrier.

Then she felt his hands on her head, tangling her hair roughly, desperately. Clinging in spite of himself.

"I — need you — Marian."

Now she wept like Barney had, unafraid of letting him see, kissing his wet face, refusing to pretend any more,

"I love you, Charles."

She took his hands, leading him to the piano stool, standing behind him, her hands on his shoulders.

"Never mind the Wagner," she said. "Play me some Chopin." ∎

Country Children

by Joyce Stranger

Inspired by an illustration by Mark Viney

Children should have lots of fun, so the pundits say.

Tell that to our little son and his friends who come to stay.

What their elders think is work these children think is play.

Morning time the chickens feed. Bring the bucket, scatter seed.

New-born piglets . . . time to meet. Watch children's faces when they greet.

The little calves, still bucket fed, fetch our son early from his bed.

Up with Dad before the dawn to see a calf that's newly born.

Lambs there are to bottle feed. Happy creatures with such greed.

Now it's time the straw to tend and make each horse a soft clean bed.

Then to gather in the sheep. Collect the eggs. The yard to sweep.

Go and play? They smile in scorn. Say city kids don't know they're born.

This isn't work, it's 'normous fun. Just you ask our little son.

Don't Give Up On Love

To save herself from pain she'd shut out the one thing in life that could bring her happiness.

By Josefine Beaumont

I WAS nine years old when my mother died in one of those senseless car accidents that never ought to happen. So, it was left to my father to raise me — and raise me he did. Save for Aggie, the housekeeper, and Mrs Harrop who came in daily, Father looked no further for assistance and, as was to be expected, we grew exceptionally close.

I adored him. He was a great big cuddly bear of a man with unruly hair that sprang from his bullet-shaped head.

His eyes were steely grey and missed nothing, his chin determined and his lips could curl into a great grin, or curl in contempt, depending upon the occasion.

Despite the loss of my mother, I knew what happiness was. It was the hours Father and I spent in the antique shop he owned, learning about the wonderful

163

things of a bygone age. Or when we walked hand-in-hand through the park on a crisp, autumn day, our feet scuffing the leaves that lay at our feet.

It was a cold, winter day, a log fire, hot toasted teacakes and a good book. My father also had a deep love of literature.

"You can keep your film stars and politicians," he scoffed derisively. "Give me a man who can write, any day.

"I tell you, lass," he went on, fixing those warm, grey eyes full upon my face and I shivered with sheer delight, "the ability to write is a gift!

"I'd give all I had to be able to string words together and for them to hold real meaning. I mean it — every penny and no mistake!"

"Every penny?" I echoed, eyes widening. "But wouldn't we be poor?"

"Poor?" The look in his eyes seemed faraway and then he shook his head wistfully and murmured, "Perhaps in money, Jessie, but we'd be richer in another way."

So I was encouraged to read, too. We waded through the classics and spent many a happy hour in lively discussion.

And my father never placed any restrictions upon the subject matter.

I've lost count of the times Aggie came across a controversial book.

She'd click her false teeth, setting my own on edge, and declare sharply, "It's not suitable reading for a young girl, Howard Armitage, and you know it!"

"And what would you know?" he'd demand, chin thrust out defiantly. "You stick to filling her stomach, woman, and I'll attend to filling her head!"

Then they'd glare at each other, neither meaning it, for Aggie had been with us for years and was just like one of the family.

WAS 13 before I realised how unhappy Father was. It was my birthday and I'd charged downstairs in a whirl of excitement to thank him for the brightly-wrapped gifts I'd found heaped upon my dressing-table. I could hear the murmur of his voice from within the study, so I opened the door.

I never forgot what I saw then.

He was standing before the marble fireplace above which hung a full-length portrait of my mother. Even from where I was standing, I could see the naked pain in his face.

He didn't notice me and I heard him mutter miserably, "I miss you, Mary. But then you know that, don't you?

"Oh, Mary." He rested his head upon the mantel. "Oh, lass . . ."

I backed away quietly and gently closed the door. I remember standing in the hall and staring blindly at the polished wood of the banister rail.

But, most of all, I remember the muffled sound of his sobs coming through the door.

I fled to the kitchen, where Aggie and Mrs Harrop were preparing lunch, and threw myself into a chair.

"And what's the matter with you, Jessica Armitage?" Aggie demanded. "Face tripping you like that and this your birthday! I should have thought you'd be over the moon, child."

"Nothing!" I replied sullenly.

"Nothing?" Aggie clicked her teeth. "Nothing put a look like that on your face, did it? Well I never. Anyway, I'm too busy preparing the colcannon for lunch and I don't want you under me feet, madam — sulky face or not!"

Colcannon was a part-Irish, part-Scottish dish of potatoes and cabbage, boiled and pounded. It was my favourite.

Mrs Harrop, though, paused in the shredding of the cabbage and asked softly, "What is it, Jessie dear?"

I lifted my eyes to meet her anxious look. Everything about Lydia Harrop was soft, her voice, skin and gently waving hair. Her large, brown eyes rested now upon my wan face.

I hadn't understood then and, to this day, I still cannot understand how her husband could have left her for another woman.

"It's Dad," I answered miserably.

"What about your dad?" She smiled softly.

So I told her what I'd seen and heard.

The look on her face was most peculiar as she whispered raggedly, "He said that? Your . . . your dad said that?"

I nodded.

She sank into a chair and, meeting Aggie's eyes, said, "I knew it. I just knew it!

"I should have left last year. I knew I should. I shouldn't have let you talk me out of it!"

"Now, Lydia, I'll have none of that talk!" Aggie commanded in her sternest voice. "You have to give him time."

"Time?" she echoed bitterly. "It's been four years, Aggie. Four years! And he still doesn't know I exist."

I watched, wide-eyed, as Aggie pointed a wooden spoon at Mrs Harrop and cried impatiently, "He's a man, Lydia, and you know what they're like.

"You have to point them in the right direction."

"And how do I do that?" Mrs Harrop demanded. "I've done all but dance naked in front of him and it's made no difference.

"I'm telling you, he'll never get over her."

As I remember, I was quite shocked at this exchange. Fancy Mrs Harrop talking about dancing naked in front of my dad!

I even stole a wary glance at Aggie, certain her face would be contorted into a look of outrage.

For Aggie didn't hold with what she darkly termed, "loose talk."

Much to my surprise, she adopted her Grandma Agnes look — the one she reserved for a child's cut knees or for illnesses and funerals.

"It could be worse," Aggie pointed out reasonably. "He could have taken up with another woman, Lydia. Think on it like that."

Six months later, it was another woman.

Mrs Hart was a widow, a small, thin woman with a permanently tight face, sleek hairdo and smart, city clothes.

I didn't like her, Aggie didn't like her and, not surprisingly, Mrs Harrop didn't like her.

Not that it mattered because, it seemed, my dad liked her enough for all of us.

I often wonder if he would have married her. But I was never ever to know.

For two days short of my fourteenth birthday, my father had a sudden and fatal heart attack.

He was 41 years old at the time.

We all went to pieces — especially Aggie. But I remember someone screaming, too, and Dr Marsden shaking me and saying firmly, "Stop it, Jessie! Stop it!"

I'd started in surprise, for I hadn't realised the screams were my own. I was bereft.

We all huddled together for comfort at the funeral and I can still clearly recall Mrs Hart's sharp features pathetically crumpled.

It made me realise that she had loved him even as we had.

The house was sold, while the antique shop was held in trust for me until I was 18.

I was sent to live with Aunt Janet and Uncle George, neither of whom liked children very much.

Not that they were unkind; far from it. But they had deliberately chosen not to have a family of their own.

It must have been very irksome to find themselves lumbered with a 14-year-old girl.

Therefore they raised no objections when, at 18, I moved out.

That same week I took over Father's shop, the antiques business being the only thing I knew.

I was young, but, if life had taught me anything at all, it was never to love anyone again.

For, love hurt. If you loved people, you'd only lose them. Who knew that better than me? I vowed never to love anyone again!

And that was how I lived.

WAS 26 when Andrew Hirst asked me to marry him. He had been coming into the shop for years — sometimes to buy, sometimes to sell. Often, he'd browse or pass the time of day with me. He taught at the local school but antiques were his hobby and, because of that, we had become friends.

It was a tentative friendship. For, always, I held back. And it was the only friendship I had made. Even I hadn't been able to harden myself against his open, kind face and easy-going manner.

He was a nice man and I liked him.

That summer he had taken a party of sixth-formers on a tour of Italy. School trips, he laughingly informed me, were the dread of the continent.

But all the time he was away I wouldn't admit to myself that I missed him.

I had never spoken to him of my past, being very adroit at evading anything which I had no desire to dwell upon.

But something of my passion for books must have shown, for, when he returned, he called into the shop with a gift for me.

It was a beautiful, fully illustrated book on Florence.

I leafed through the pages, unable to stop myself blushing furiously.

"It's lovely, Andrew," I told him gratefully. "Thank you."

"I knew you'd like it, Jessica," he told me simply.

He never called me Jessie — it was always Jessica.

Still in a fluster, I made coffee in the small percolator I kept in the back room of the shop.

When I handed him his cup, he perched gingerly upon a Louis XIV chair and said to me, "You'd love Florence, Jessica. You'll have to go there yourself one day."

What he didn't realise was that I had been there.

It wasn't often I let the past in, but for a fleeting moment, I winged back in time.

It was the summer of my eleventh year and my father and I spent three glorious weeks in Florence. We had done and seen all the usual touristy things.

Now, it all seemed so very long ago — another life almost.

Then I saw Andrew studying me, a tender smile in his eyes. There was a long, long silence before he said to me, so very gently, "I have grown to love you, Jessica."

SO this was how love came to me in that small shop with the weak shafts of sunshine spilling on to the carpeted floor. It came so gently, easily — not forcing its way in. It came holding out the hand of friendship.

And how it frightened me!

"Don't say that!" I cried sharply, not wanting to hear any more.

"Why ever not? It's the truth."

I jumped to my feet, closing my eyes against the truth that was causing me to tremble.

I didn't want any of it — to miss him when he was away or to hope that, each time the doorbell of the shop pinged, I would see him standing, framed in the doorway.

But, most of all, I didn't want to be hurt again. Not ever!

He had no right, I told myself angrily, to say such a thing! Or to make me experience what I was feeling in that moment of time.

Who gave him the right to knock down the wall I had built around my heart and feelings?

When his hands rested lightly upon my shoulders, I stiffened. It had been years since I'd allowed anyone physical contact with me.

When he looked down into my face, I closed my eyes tightly, for I didn't want to see what I knew would be revealed in his kindly face.

"Will you marry me, Jessica?" he asked, drawing me against the hairy tweed of his jacket. "Will you?"

His jacket smelled faintly of pipe tobacco and aftershave.

I lay against it, like an imprisoned bird, listening to the steady thump of his heart, and the fear subsided, the trembling abated.

I laid my face against his chest and suddenly thought how good it felt. Safe and warm.

All the pent-up pain seemed to ebb away with the silent tears that coursed down my face. His arms held me close. His voice was low and soothing when he said, "Tell me, Jessica. Tell me all about it, my love."

I did just that, leaving out none of my pain and confusion.

And, when I could say no more, he said sorrowfully, "Oh, Jessica!" and I knew then that I could love this man.

But not yet. First, I had to lay my ghosts.

*　　*　　*　　*

That night, I sat down and wrote to Aggie, praying she would forgive the unanswered letters and the years of silence.

And, the next morning, instead of opening the shop, I paid a long, overdue visit to Lydia Harrop.

168

It took a while to find her for she had remarried. But she hadn't changed much, she was still the same soft-all-over Mrs Harrop of my childhood.

Her husband was a very pleasant man, a few years older than her. I could see at a glance his deep affection for Lydia.

It made me like him all the more.

When my visit was over, she walked me to the car and we stood in silence, our eyes meeting.

Then she said wistfully, "I loved your father, Jessica."

I smiled sadly as I replied, "I know."

She glanced quickly at her home, then said defensively, "Arnold's a good man."

"Yes," I agreed. "He is."

I paused a moment before asking tentatively, "Are you . . . are you happy, Lydia?"

"Oh, yes," she replied with conviction. "I never thought I would be again, but I am."

I was glad, so glad that she had found happiness.

As I got into the car, a sudden thought struck me. "Whatever happened to Mrs Hart?" I asked.

"Cathleen?" Lydia smiled. "It's uncanny you should ask that, Jessie, because, only this morning, I had a letter from her.

"She lives in America now, you know. She married a very wealthy businessman."

"You kept in touch?" I asked, greatly surprised.

"Oh, yes." Lydia smiled softly again. "It's strange, Jessie, but I grew very fond of her.

"She . . . she loved your father very much, too, you know. I . . . I think she would have made him very happy."

Through a faint veil of tears, I started up the car engine.

Lydia leaned forward and asked anxiously, "You will keep in touch, won't you, Jessie?"

I nodded blindly, too moved to speak, and drove away.

On the way home, I thought about Lydia and Cathleen Hart both loving the same man.

They had been rivals once, but were firm friends now. It was amazing how life worked out.

They had both genuinely loved my father, yet they had not been afraid to give life — and love — a second chance.

I knew then that like them, I would never be afraid to love again.

TEN years have now passed. Sometimes, I think about all that I almost missed. I remember the long nights in my lonely bed, the long days bereft of human warmth, and it frightens me a little. I think anxiously of how I almost missed the love of a man who has come to mean everything to me, of the children I almost never had.

There's eight-year-old Howard Andrew, named after my father and husband, seven-year-old Louise whose smile lights up my life and three-year-old Jenny whose laughter lifts my spirits until they soar.

Aggie lives with us now. My children call her Nana. She pets them, scolds them, fusses and loves them.

It is all so very familiar to me — the wheel, it seems, has come full circle.

But she is very old now, and many of her conversations begin with, "Do you remember, Jessie . . .?"

And I do – I love to remember, now. I let the past in, no longer running and hiding from it.

I no longer fear the memories, but cling lovingly to them as they should be cherished.

I hope that my children will grow tall, strong and brave; that they'll meet life and all that is in it, face to face.

For that is how it should be lived.

But, most of all, I hope that, should life or love ever knock them down, as often happens, they will have the courage to pick up the pieces and go forward seeking a better, happier future. ■

Such Different Dreams

Over the years our hopes and ambitions had changed so much. But then so had we . . .

by Isobel Stewart

AM a thirty-five-year-old mother of two." Sounds like the start of a letter on a problem page, doesn't it?

But — no, my husband isn't unfaithful to me, he doesn't drink, he doesn't beat me and he gives me as much housekeeping money as he can. We love each other, we laugh together — we have a good marriage.

I really mean that.

So why do I stand at my kitchen sink this fine morning, and say these words aloud?

"I am a thirty-five-year old mother of two." Because that is indeed what I am. I love my children, I love them dearly. But suddenly I find myself wondering where she went to, the girl I was 10 years ago. And where did he go to, the young man Steve was?

The people we were yesterday are not the people we are today. And the saddest thing of all is that I didn't even see them go. I couldn't even say goodbye.

It must have happened so slowly, imperceptibly, that I have only just realised they have gone.

T HE house is quiet now, and Steve is off to do his house calls before morning surgery. There is some kind of virus going about at the moment, affecting lots of children — little Johnny down the road for one — so I know just how busy Steve will be. I make myself a cup of coffee, and sit down in my bright, sunny kitchen, and I think about those young people of 10 years ago.

Margy and Steve. So young, so much in love, with so many dreams. Steve had just finished medical school, and I was newly qualified as a nurse. We were full of dreams, full of ideals.

Maybe we'd go to Central America or to China, as a medical missionary team. Maybe Steve would go into research, and I'd help him. Maybe he'd specialise. Maybe . . .

Oh, there were so many dreams, so many possibilities. But what I really remember from these days is less easy to put into words.

There was a sort of magic, a circle of enchantment, that surrounded and enclosed us. We just had to look at each other, to touch hands, and the magic was there. That is what has gone.

The love is there, steady and true, but — that magic, that circle of enchantment, belonged to the people we were yesterday, the people who have gone now.

My coffee is finished and I take my cup to the sink. The spring sunshine is warming the washing on the line. Iain's white coats hang beside Sarah's minute jeans and Ian's bigger ones.

Steve's pyjamas are next to my nightie, and two small pairs of pyjamas, one with red hearts and one with blue hearts, are beside them.

I am a foolish and ungrateful woman, I tell myself sternly. I love my children . . . they and Steve are my world. And of course things change, people change. But — so much?

I'm perfectly content, really, and I know Steve likes being a family doctor, it's just that suddenly the difference in our lives now seems rather sad.

I couldn't begin to imagine living without my children, but they've certainly changed everything.

My day is going to be busy, as it always is, and there is no more time to stand in my kitchen indulging in foolish regrets. I'm on duty at the tuckshop at school in the middle of the morning, and I have to hurry now to get there in time.

It isn't my most favourite job, but I know that Sarah likes to see me there, taking my turn.

And so dutifully, I do just that . . .

"That is my mummy," Sarah says importantly, bringing a red-haired, freckled, little boy up to me as I stand selling crisps to the children.

"Mummy, this is Peter, he's my very best friend."

"Hello, Peter," I greet the new best friend, and I wonder if Sarah will tell me what happened to last week's best friend.

I see her go off, with a group of friends, and she gives a friendly nod — and suddenly this little girl of mine is so like my grandmother that I find myself almost laughing aloud.

Shopping on the way home takes the rest of the morning, and I'm only just ready with toasted cheese for Steve and me when he hurries in, abstracted, his mind already on his busy afternoon.

I know that old Mrs Brown's ulcer and Beth Johnson's baby's croup — which we talk about over our toasted cheese — are top of his priorities at this moment, and I don't mind that. I can understand, having been a nurse.

Afternoons are always too short, and I know there isn't really time to do much to Emma's princess costume for her class play, but I know, too, that she'll be disappointed if I don't even begin it.

"Are you sure I'll look like a princess?" she'd asked me doubtfully at breakfast this morning. "Do you think my hair will grow really long in two weeks?" I'd looked at the two little bunches of brown hair standing out from her head.

"Not really long, no," I'd replied carefully and honestly. "It won't hang down over your shoulders. But it will be longer than it is now."

I'd hugged her, and kissed her furrowed little brow. "But you will look like a princess, I know that," I told her, and meant it.

When I pick her up at school that afternoon, she reminds me she needs trainers and we rush down to the shops and get them, blue for Emma and little yellow ones for Ian.

I drop Sarah off at her ballet class, and not for the first time I congratulate myself on co-ordinating these two journeys.

I have an hour before she will be ready, so I hurry back home to get dinner organised.

AND suddenly, in the middle of peeling potatoes, I realise that I am happy. This is my life, this is my reality, and — this is me, this 35-year-old mother of two. I am Steve's wife, Ian's and Emma's mother, and that's how I want it. I don't really want to be a medical missionary in China, I don't want to be Marie Curie, I'm very happy to be the wife of a GP in a small town.

And yet at the same time, I know that I have just a tinge of regret for those people we were yesterday, just a hint of nostalgia for that magic, that enchantment that we once shared.

Steve phones while the children are in the bath, and says he wants to stay at the hospital for a bit, to see how Mrs Brown is.

"Don't hold back the meal for me," he advises, "but I'll try to be home before the children go to bed."

I'm fond of Mrs Brown, and I've been worried about her, so I'm glad he'll be with her.

I wonder, as I run back upstairs holding a wet baby, how doctor's wives managed before microwave ovens were invented. Maybe, I tell myself with a wry smile, I need my microwave oven more than I need magic nowadays.

Somehow or other, this leads me to the thought that perhaps it's up to me to recapture the magic.

Perhaps, I tell myself, if I can get myself organised to do a refresher course I might be able to take a part-time job at the hospital. There's no reason why plans and dreams shouldn't still be a part of our lives.

THE children and I eat, and clear up, then Sarah watches her favourite TV programme, with the usual disappointment when it's finished. I check her homework — Sarah doesn't really get any yet, but she likes to be a bit grown up, so we always do her "homework" too.

I read another two chapters of "The Wind In The Willows," and first Sarah falls asleep, then Ian.

The house is quiet, and it's nearly dark when Steve comes home. While he has dinner, he tells me that Mrs Brown is going to be all right, and I say I'll call in at the hospital to see her.

We drink our coffee in the lounge, to the strains of an old Beatles record we've always loved — but haven't listened to for years.

We sit on the couch together, and listen to the Famous Four asking if we'll still need them and feed them when they're 64. And then they start on "Yesterday", and I sit down on the rug at Steve's feet, and lean my head against his knee, and I think, warmly, happily, that maybe this is different, and we're different, from 10 years ago — but it's still very pleasant.

Steve's hand is stroking my hair, and I hum the words, softly — "I believe in yesterday."